MW00834168

Just A Pinch of Magic

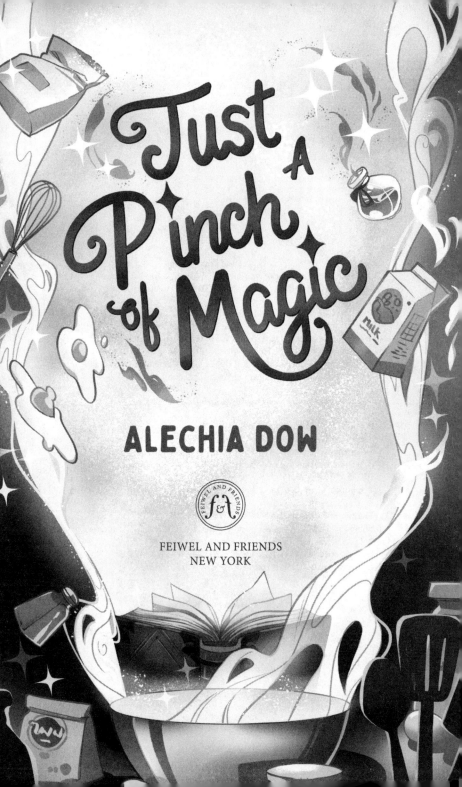

Just A Pinch of Magic

ALECHIA DOW

FEIWEL AND FRIENDS
NEW YORK

A Feiwel and Friends Book
An imprint of Macmillan Publishing Group, LLC
120 Broadway, New York, NY 10271 • mackids.com

Copyright © 2023 by Alechia Dow. All rights reserved.

Our books may be purchased in bulk for promotional, educational, or business use. Please contact your local bookseller or the Macmillan Corporate and Premium Sales Department at (800) 221-7945 ext. 5442 or by email at MacmillanSpecialMarkets@macmillan.com.

Library of Congress Cataloging-in-Publication Data

Names: Dow, Alechia, author.
Title: Just a pinch of magic / Alechia Dow.
Description: First edition. | New York : Feiwel & Friends, 2023. |
    Audience: Ages 8–12. | Audience: Grades 4–6. | Summary: Twelve-
    year-old Wini and Kal, two young enchanters from different magical
    families, team up to save their small town from a love spell gone wrong,
    which one of them cast.
Identifiers: LCCN 2022052622 | ISBN 9781250829115 (hardcover)
Subjects: CYAC: Magic—Fiction. | Friendship—Fiction. | Fantasy. |
    LCGFT: Fantasy fiction. | Novels.
Classification: LCC PZ7.1.D6836 Ju 2023 | DDC [Fic]—dc23
LC record available at https://lccn.loc.gov/2022052622

First edition, 2023
Book design by Meg Sayre
Feiwel and Friends logo designed by Filomena Tuosto
Printed in the United States of America by Lakeside Book Company,
Harrisburg, Virginia

ISBN 978-1-250-82911-5
1 3 5 7 9 10 8 6 4 2

To the librarians, teachers,

students, bakers, and

curse-breakers, you are magical.

And to Catherine and Bernice,

thanks for the loving memories.

Recipe Journal of Winifred Mosley

BLUEBERRY MUFFIN CAKE

(Because you should start your day right, okay?)

Ingredients:

1/2 cup butter, at room temperature

1/2 cup sugar

1/2 cup brown sugar

2 large eggs

2 teaspoons baking powder

1/2 teaspoon salt

1 teaspoon vanilla extract

2 cups all-purpose flour

2/3 cup milk

2 1/2 cups blueberries (I use frozen because I like my
   bread to be purply fantastic.)

1 teaspoon cinnamon for topping

1/3 cup brown sugar mixed with cinnamon for
   topping (set aside)

How to make:

1. Preheat the oven to 375°F. Prepare a standard
   loaf pan by coating the sides in nonstick spray OR

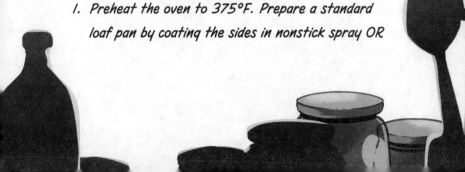

vegetable oil and a light dusting of flour. Spray's easier, though.

2. In a mixing bowl, beat together the butter and both sugars until well combined and sorta fluffy.

3. Add the eggs one at a time, scraping the sides and bottom of the bowl and beating well after each addition.

4. Add the baking powder, salt, and vanilla.

5. Alternate adding the flour with the milk, stirring gently just to combine. Scrape the bottom and sides of the bowl.

6. Add the blueberries to the batter, stirring just to combine using a rubber spatula—and before you even think it, YES, BUY ONE. They're awesome.

7. Pour batter into the pan, smoothing it with that handy-dandy spatula.

8. Sprinkle the loaf with the brown sugar-cinnamon mixture until perfectly coated.

9. Bake for about an hour, until a toothpick inserted into the middle comes out clean.

10. Remove from the oven and let it cool in the pan for an hour before eating.

11. Yield: UM, ONE PERSON? I suppose you could share it. I mean, if you want to be nice or whatever.

1

Wini

My nerves flutter around like powdered sugar just before it lands on top of a warm chocolate soufflé. The wind howls outside my window, promising a storm soon. I'd better get a move on.

"Pen to paper, words to cook, close and seal my special book." My recipe journal whooshes shut and seals itself as I take another bite of the Fabulous Financier I smuggled from my family's bakery, Wayward Sentiments Café & Sweetery. The almond cake—which is sheer perfection, if I do say so myself—is supposed to make me feel unstoppable and successful, but it hasn't kicked in yet. I really hope it does soon. Because tonight, with a little bit of magic and all the talent I can muster, I'm going to make a dream come true.

At least I hope I can. In all honesty, I've never done anything like this before.

But failure is not an option.

I'm wearing my best vintage, plus-size thrift treasures: knee-high boots that go perfectly with the new fifties blue-and-red plaid dress I found in the clearance bin. I buckle the belt on the emerald-green trench coat that makes me feel like a devious girl on a mission. Of course, I *am* a devious girl on a mission, but I add a multicolored scarf to soften the image.

This is armor for the most dreaded battle of the season: I'm going to my very first Thursday night football game, where everyone and their mom will be doing whatever people do at football games. Honeycrisp Hill loves community time and a contact sport.

The sun set a little bit ago, and all that's left is the pale pink glow of twilight. The rest of the shops down the block sport pumpkins and leaf garlands that flutter as the October air sends chilly gusts up and down Main Street. A smile creeps to my lips. Fall's my favorite. Everything seems a bit wonderful, a bit possible, this time of year.

I adjust my glasses, take a deep breath . . . and walk right into my dad, who's carrying a fifty-pound sack of flour like it's a bag of Halloween candy. A haze of magic spirals around him—a strength spell to help him carry all the heavy flour and sugar into the bakery. My purse nearly falls off my shoulder and I stumble slightly before correcting myself.

His dark eyes lock on mine. "Where are you going?"

"Uh, you know . . ." I raise my chin slowly. "Just going to the game. Being normal. Acting my age. Like you keep telling me to do."

He lets out a howl of laughter that cuts through my fear of getting caught like a hot spoon through ice cream. "You should ease into it, you know? Games are a big step." Dad and Aunt Maddie don't go to the games, preferring to seize the perfect opportunity to clean the shop without any customers around.

"It won't be so bad. I can drink hot chocolate and leave anytime. Besides," I say, stepping around him, avoiding eye contact, "I'm going to make new friends."

He eyes my adorable outfit. "Friends from *this* century?"

I make a face. "Says the guy who has a bow tie collection."

He shakes his head with a small chuckle. "Okay, okay. Just have fun. Message me when you get there, okay?"

"Mm-hm, yup. Love you, too, Dad. Gotta go!" I rush past him, putting in my earbuds. Stevie Wonder's "Sir Duke" makes the best soundtrack on my short walk through the town to the school.

The thing about Honeycrisp Hill, Rhode Island, is that it's small. Ridiculously small. Everyone knows one another. There's no such thing as privacy here. And this is the safest, most magical place on Earth, which is why no one bats an eye at a twelve-year-old—which is nearly a teenager, which means I'm on my way to adulthood, thank you very much—walking alone.

As I tread into the town square (it's actually a trapezoid), complete with a statue in the center named Derrick, I notice Ms. Chavers at the same time she notices me. Her eyes and mouth go wide.

"You!" she spits out. Even though I can't hear her, I know the sound well. Thankfully, Stevie's keeping me cozy and safe.

Ms. Chavers, the grumpiest resident of Honeycrisp Hill, has been my enemy for a few years now. It all happened one day in a grocery store line. See, there was only one pint of fresh strawberries left. And I had my hands on them. I'd planned on making strawberry shortcake—you know, the perfect summer treat—when she grabbed the container from me. So I did what anyone who has their dreams suddenly crushed does . . . I pointed out the shop window and said, "Oh my goodness, is that Tom Hanks?"

Fact: His Meg Ryan rom-coms are the only DVDs at the public library, and they're always checked out. Ms. Chavers works at the library. Coincidence? I think not.

In the moment of distraction, her grip loosened and I snatched the strawberries and made my escape. Since that fateful day, every time she sees me, a deep, withering glare etches onto her face. The drama is real, but I'm not gonna lie: The shortcake was worth it.

I scurry away with a cheeky wink. I wave quickly at Derrick the statue and Mr. Collins, his living keeper, who is currently sweeping errant leaves away from the base of Derrick's stone feet. Mr. Collins glares my way.

Because the other thing about Honeycrisp Hill is that *everyone* here is a bit weird. A bit . . . off. And grumpy, especially to me. Before I was born, my birth mom, Coraline—who I never even met!—cast a curse on the entire town. No one knows why or even how she did it, but one thing was certain afterward: Any enchanter who was there when the curse fell upon the town can't leave without losing their magic forever. Including Aunt Maddie and Dad, which is why no one blames them.

Nope. They blame *me*.

I look just like her, my magic's just as potent, and I was born outside of town, so I have the freedom to leave. It makes sense that I'm the easiest target for their scorn. I only wish I wasn't.

Anyway, there's nothing I can do about any of that. No matter how many times I apologize, or how many times I research breaking curses, I'm just a kid in a small magical town, going to a football game.

A very crowded football game.

When I pass the first of my classmates in the parking lot, I'm met with stares.

"It's Black Betty Crocker."

"Stay far, far away from her."

"*Witch.*"

I'm not a witch. I'm an enchanter, just like them.

A food enchanter, to be exact. Some enchanters make their magic through art, some through weather, nature, books—different specialties that focus and amplify our magic. We all have basic magic: Spells we can cast to move things, lock things. Small actions that don't require time and are simple and specific—like the one I plan to use tonight. Extraction is an enchanter's bread and butter.

The thought of bread makes me hungry again.

As I weave through my classmates, whose older siblings probably play on the team, and their parents, they whisper in surprise at seeing me there. I smile anxiously. I'm used to their judgment by now.

This cursed town loves a villain.

Coraline's curse didn't just make it impossible for them to leave, it also accidentally killed someone. So not only is she a "witch" (an enchanter who went bad), she's also a murderer. Our last name is still a dirty word around here—and the bakery's about to close because of it.

I will change that. I have to. That's why I'm here.

After buying a jumbo hot chocolate, I message Dad that I arrived and then turn around, my new boots squelching on the pavement, as parents and teachers stream by. One of them is my target tonight: Mrs. Mabel Jenkins, home economics teacher and all-around foodie. She's been married to Principal Edison Jenkins for forty years or something. When they pass each other in the hall, it's like time stands still. Their fingers touch and the energy in the air picks up and frizzles. If I weren't such a sucker for love, I might find it gross.

But my spell relies heavily on the Jenkinses and their big hearts.

Cheers ring out as I amble through the grass toward the stands. The stadium lights blur my vision and I squint, losing sight of Mrs. Jenkins, only to catch her cackle of a laugh that guides me onward.

Everything is so extreme here. Noise? Too loud. Lights? Too bright. Cheerleading outfits? Too adorable. People? Too many. Dad was right, football games are a big step. This might be more enjoyable if everything just chilled out a bit more. And maybe if there was some soothing music playing. And instead of football, it was a baking competition. In a tent. A warm tent that smells of fresh bread and dreams. Also, some kind judges who really just want the best for the bakers.

I'm losing track here.

Cheerleaders arrange themselves on the field to applause. They're shouting about something, possibly team spirit and the beginning of the season. I don't really know. All I do know is that these games are the only time everyone wants to pretend we're just like normal people. No magic—especially on the field. Just good ol' American fun. Blech.

I manage to squeeze in right behind Mrs. Jenkins and Principal Jenkins. People maneuver around and away from me as if my close proximity will bring them uncertain doom. Thankfully the Jenkinses don't notice.

Focus, I tell myself. If I get this done fast, I can get out of here before we're expected to chant something and I mess up. And I'm not even going to think about the fact that what I'm about to do isn't strictly *legal*, either. It doesn't matter. I don't have a choice.

When the cheering pauses, I lean over. *Play it cool. Don't be weird. Be one with the lies.*

"Hello, Mrs. Jenkins!" I sort of shout at her.

She turns around slowly, with a wobbly grin. "Winifred Mosley. I'm excited to see you outside the bakery. Look, Edison, it's Winifred."

Principal Jenkins's eyebrows nearly melt into his wrinkled forehead. "Ms. Mosley, I didn't know you liked . . . things."

I try to smile but end up doing something awkward with my entire face. "I like all kinds of things. And I've got . . . you know, spirit. For life." Ugh, what does that even mean?

Principal Jenkins nods, but I can tell he's already try-ing to end this conversation with me before it starts. I understand. But I have to press on. I can't fail, not when I'm this close.

"Mrs. Jenkins, I was wondering something."

Her head tilts to the side, jostling some of her big curls loose. "What's that, honey?"

"So you know . . . I'm here by myself and, uh, it would be great to be here with my dad and maybe he could be here with me, and um . . . someone special. They could be sharing hot chocolates and . . . a blanket. Because it's a bit cold, huh?" Could I be any weirder? I need to get to the point. "Like you two . . . How did you meet?"

The trick to a quick extraction is to simplify. If I get the targets to talk about love, I won't have to wade through their other emotions, making it easier to extract. Of course, getting people to talk about love can be awkward.

"That's a strange question, Winifred," Principal Jen-kins says.

I'm losing him. Time to turn on the charm.

"I guess . . ." I begin, over the rising chittering in the stands, "that I just want Dad to have someone special like you two do. He's always working, and he needs to be happy . . . I think he forgot how to, you know, talk to people." I'm rather impressed with my acting here—it really sounds like I mean it.

"Is the bakery still struggling?" Principal Jenkins asks, lips pressed firmly together in a sympathetic smile.

I nod. Sadly, it's very much struggling. Barring a miracle, we'll have to close it soon.

Not if I can help it, though.

Mrs. Jenkins's face softens. "I'm sorry, dear." I know she means it, too. She was friends with my grandma Bernice and helped at the bakery sometimes, even though she's not a food enchanter. I think she's a thread enchanter; she can turn thread into blankets and clothes that never age, never shrink, always fit, and always adjust to the exact temperature your body needs. She sells her designs at a shop downtown. "Now, I shouldn't be telling you this because you don't need to be in grown folks' business, but the key to love is making someone laugh. That's what your dad needs to do. Laughter solves everything."

I let my head drop a little, abashed. "Is that what you did? Made Principal Jenkins laugh when you met?"

Principal Jenkins tosses his wife a look. It's that look people get when they're reminded how lucky they are to have found their match. The kind of love that makes a person's stomach warm, flip, and dip. That's what Grandma Bernice called it. A flippy-dippy love. It's rare and precious, and the Jenkinses radiate it.

I mutter the extraction spell under my breath while

they're still looking at each other: *"Heart and mind, body and soul, shimmer bright what hides in sight."*

The air around us explodes in color that only I, the caster, can see. Fear is a greenish yellow. Calm is the blue of water gently bubbling in a brook. Anger is bright orange with hints of red . . . kind of like the surface of the sun. And love . . . love is purple. The stronger the color, the stronger the emotion.

"Would you believe we were high school sweethearts?" Mrs. Jenkins recalls. "One day I was walking up the steps to school and this boy with his head held high and mighty stopped in front of me. I started to walk past him, just standing there like a statue, when he cleared his throat." She laughs, her eyes far off as if seeing into the past. "And he asked me, in a voice too deep to be real, if he could carry my books. He had me laughing so hard!"

Principal Jenkins shakes his head. "I was trying to impress you. I couldn't speak right after that for a good day."

"Boy!" Mrs. Jenkins giggles, hitting his shoulder.

I watch with awe as the most lovely, sparkly blackberry purple swirls around us. I've never seen it so beautiful. I mean, how would I? No one in my immediate family is in love.

Quickly, I unlatch the vial in my jacket pocket. I

shimmy my shoulder, causing my bag to drop between the Jenkinses and me. When they both scoop down to pick it up, I swing my arm out to capture some of the love floating around us.

I'm *definitely* breaking enchantment law right now. Viewing emotions is one thing, but taking some is a big no-no. If everyone just took emotions willy-nilly, the world would be chaos—or so I've been told by every single adult my entire life.

Normally, emotions can only be bought from a licensed seller. But I can't afford the legal route; neither can the bakery. And my spell to *save* the bakery requires it. It's a risk, I know, because if I take too much, I might affect them—make their love a little less strong—which would draw attention, which would then cause the Enchantment Agency to investigate, and that's the last thing I need.

I play it safe and fill the vial a third of the way. I only need one drop anyway.

I finish the spell, leaving the air as normal and boring as before. "Thank you for sharing your story with me," I say to Mrs. Jenkins, whose eyes glimmer in the bright lights. I begin taking a step back. I can go home! No football or cheering. Success is within reach!

"Winifred Mosley, you better focus on yourself and not your father. You're a lovely girl; you gotta let people see that. Make some friends." Mrs. Jenkins smiles like she's told me something I haven't heard before.

Be yourself.

Act your age.

Stop criticizing the "culinary value" of school lunches.

You're gonna get sick if you eat that much chocolate.

It's like people never get enough of telling me how to live. Grandma Bernice never did that. She told me that I was going to be just fine, even if I've got the soul of an eighty-year-old. I like crackling fireplaces, vintage clothes, and fresh scones with tea. Who, in this teeny town of Honeycrisp Hill, would want to be friends with *me*?

"Right, right. I should get going . . ."

"You're not staying for the game?" Principal Jenkins throws his hands up. I can tell these things mean a lot to him.

"I'm sure it'll be great. The Sharks are going to win!"

"That's the other team," Principal Jenkins explains with a small, exasperated shake of his head.

"I meant us. I mean we'll win. Who are we again?"

"The Lions!" some of the surrounding people respond, their voices edged with annoyance.

"Yes! The Lions, that's it." I grin, but Principal Jenkins grimaces. "Bye. See you Monday! Thanks again!"

I step over some fans who are casting a spell to make

the cold, metal bleachers warmer. Their spell doesn't sound quite right, but people don't like when I correct them. Especially adults. I look away and make eye contact with a pair of two very old, very gray men who are dressed in colorful sports jerseys. They drink from their team thermoses and give me the stink eye. Football really is a subculture, huh?

I take off just as the teams start to play, finishing up my hot chocolate on the way. All in all, I'd say this mission was a success.

Now . . . to cast the spell.

2
Kal

I'm shelving a book while listening (and shaking my butt) to Della's newest album, *Heart Crushing Madness*, A.K.A. one certified bop after another, when there's a tap on my shoulder. I slip my headphones off, replacing Della's luscious voice with the heavy pounding of my heart. My face has to be beet red.

But when I see who it is, my embarrassment transforms into loathing.

This kid from my school—or former school as of today—Will, stands there, blue eyes squinting in the fluorescent light, sniffing at the dusty air. We're in the nine-hundreds section, the most noncirculating, hardly cleaned, musty area of our library where the coin collection books live.

I shift on my feet as Will gazes up at me. He's at least a whole head shorter than I am, and yet he makes *me* feel small. Maybe it's the air of impatience of a popular kid used to people doing what he wants.

He likely doesn't remember last year when I made confetti cupcakes for our class and he pretended to find a hair in his. He started chanting "Nasty! Nasty!" and had everyone throw their cupcakes away. I cried in the bathroom for an hour.

And now, here he is, on my last day in the school library, standing there like he's entitled to my time. "Do you have books on the Sears Tower?"

My traitorous mouth blurts, "Erm . . . in Italy?"

His eyebrows lift, a sneer curling his gross, pink lips. "No, like in Chicago?"

I shake my head. I knew that. UGH. Why is my mouth so silly? "Yeah, come on." I try to keep the frustration from my tone as I lead him over to the seven hundreds. We stop in front of the architecture stacks and I pull out two books on Chicago monuments and Willis Tower (worth noting it's no longer even called Sears Tower, so in your face, Will). They're up too high but I refuse to take them down for him. I smirk in his face.

His head falls back with a scowl as I scamper off, leaving him on tiptoes. He is never going to reach those books. My work here is done.

I step into the school librarian's office and glance at the fan art of popular YA books. I wave goodbye to the Darkling before tripping over a frayed computer wire that's supposed to be taped to the tiles. Normally I'd tell maintenance, for the millionth time, that it was a hazard, but they wouldn't listen and anyway . . . I'm leaving.

My heart feels a bit broken even thinking about it. But I'm also excited. New possibilities. New people.

Enchantment.

All my life, Dad wouldn't allow it. Said it was too dangerous in Boston, where our kind need to be kept hidden. Just like in 95 percent of the world.

But that's about to change.

Kathy, the head librarian, clutches her denim dress as she rushes over to me. "Oh, Kal, you on your way out already?"

I try to smile. "Yeah."

Kathy pats me on the back. "I'm gonna miss you, kiddo. Promise you'll write and let us know how you're doing."

Kathy's been the mom I always wanted for this past year of junior high. She has her own kids but she helps me with my homework when Dad's working late and sometimes takes me out to dinner when food's scarce in the house. Dad's been trying to cut it in the non-magical world—which is everywhere but haven cities like Honeycrisp Hill—my entire life. He wanted to prove to himself that his writing didn't need magic to be successful, and I think that's cool. But, finally, he's ready to stop denying that part of himself, and I think that's even cooler.

Tears suddenly slide down my cheeks. "I'll call you once things settle down, I promise."

"You better . . ." Her voice cracks, and I hug her just a little tighter. Her fluffy white hair feels like a pillow in the crook of my neck.

The rest of our goodbye passes in a blur. There's love between us, but also guilt. Part of me is mad at myself for not telling her my secret about magic, but another part of me knows you just can't share that kind of stuff with non-magical people. Besides, there's no time to feel bad about anything. I'm about to embark on a fresh start. A new path. Finally, Dad and I can be, I don't know, a family. We can do whatever normal families do.

That thought sticks with me as I pull out my red pleather jacket from my locker for the last time. No more lonely nights and empty refrigerators. I'll finally have a normal life.

When I take one last look at the library, I know that I'm losing this little world where I felt safe and loved, but I'm gaining so much more. I put on my headphones to continue listening to Della's album as I step out of this haven and into the world.

As I walk over the wet lawn of the giant funeral home a few blocks away from our teeny apartment, I pull a bag of doughnut holes I bought before school out of my jacket pocket. Ambulances screech in the distance, cutting through the music, and for a second, I think I might actually miss Boston. It's not as exciting as New York, Dad's hometown, but it's fun.

This is home. *Was* home. I can't wait to go to Honeycrisp Hill.

Dad jogs up behind me, pulling off my headphones in the process.

"Hey, you didn't wait for me. You know you aren't supposed to walk home from the library alone." His thick city accent makes me feel warm despite the dwindling temperature. I smile at him, hoping he can see how excited I am for our great new adventure.

He's in his black suit, the one he wears when he's trying to look like a professional, and there are rings around his eyes. Despite these things, he's still smiling.

For so long, it's just been the two of us. Though it's mostly felt like *one* of us since he's never around. It's hard to be okay with that, but I'm trying. He's giving us what I've always wanted now.

"I figured you were busy," I say as he eyes my doughnut holes and then snatches one before I can shove them both into my mouth. I let out a growl in response. "Hey!"

Between bites, he shoots me one of those defeated looks. "You're going to like Honeycrisp Hill; everyone does. There's only a handful of cities across this world that are just for magic people under the Enchantment Agency's protection. You can be yourself there."

"The Enchantment Agency?" I cock an eyebrow. I've never heard of it before, but it seems like something I should know about.

Dad wipes the powdered sugar from his fingers. "Enchanters have lived in this world since the beginning of time, but it wasn't until the 1700s that we were allowed to designate cities just for us. One of them was . . ."

I start tuning him out. Don't get me wrong, I like history, but my dad doesn't say anything with pizzazz. He just says stuff in this monotone voice that makes me want to fall asleep.

"So you're sure I'll like it there?" I cut in. Nerves— good nerves—bubble in the pit of my stomach.

He huffs, shaking his head at my lack of attention. "It's safe."

And that's the end of the discussion, I guess. Dad either says a lot or a little.

His magic medium is words. It's why he's a journalist. Words bend their will to him. He can manipulate them into articles, stories, portals . . . So by extension, I must be able to, too. Mediums are genetic, after all. Though I've never had any training in it, Dad assured me that I'm an enchanter just like him—there's a special test enchanter nurses run when enchanter children are born and apparently I passed it. Yet, unlike him, I can't legally do magic yet. He'd flip if I tried. Enchanters get arrested if they expose magic to humans outside of haven cities, even by mistake.

"I *finally* get to learn magic, though, right?" Finally, *finally*, I get to use this sparkly, weird feeling that's been cooped up inside of me for my entire life.

He stops to regard me as cars rush by on the street beside us. The streetlamp encompasses him, making the shadows under his eyes darker and his skin paler. We couldn't look more different.

I was an accidental baby. When my dad went to his first college party, he had way too much fun and met the most beautiful girl in the world, so he says. And they had me.

Lachlan Ian Clarke, a young, queer man from the big city, was just figuring out his life when he was ousted from his wealthy, well-to-do family and became a dad.

He gave up everything to move here and raise me while attending Boston University. He really wanted a kid, much to his mother's disappointment, while my mom, Zamira, who was studying abroad from Chile, decided she really didn't.

They're still friends. She pops in every few months with a tan acquired from whatever faraway location she's visited lately, bearing extremely odd gifts like a cactus from Argentina or a Peruvian panpipe. It was actually a blast learning to play that once I got the hang of it. We aren't a family, though. She's more of an acquaintance.

The only other family I have is in New York City. I've gone there a few times, but Dad's mom isn't too keen on me. She wants me to be a young lady who is respectful, never rocks the boat, and bears the Clarke name with pride and dignity. She wanted to send me to some fancy boarding school overseas, but Dad wasn't about it. Since neither of us did what she wanted, we're well and truly cut off.

That's why we're a *wee* bit poor.

"All the kids in the regular school are enchanters, but school just to learn enchantment is on the weekends." And then he does that twitchy thing with his shoulders. He only does that when he's about to tell me something bad. "Kal . . ."

"Nope!" I shout and bolt across the grass. "No crap news, only excitement and fun from here on out."

My dad starts jogging to keep up. "Will you stop it?"

"No way!" I turn the corner down the alley to our apartment and nearly trip on a pizza box that sadly wasn't ours. My hands dart into my backpack, rifling through my candy wrappers, wads of chewed-up gum balled between wax paper, and my retro collection of exactly ninety-six fruity-smelling crayons, but my keys are gone.

My dad catches up, dangling them between two fingers and laughing between pants.

I narrow my eyes. "How?" But I already know the answer. *Enchanting.* He's a pro at it. With only a few mumbled words under his breath, he can move things.

He sticks the key in the lock and holds the door open for me. With a sigh, I enter first. I let my backpack drop to the floor as I walk into the hallway—and stop dead in my tracks.

The apartment is a skyline created from towers of boxes. All of our worldly possessions are packed and prepared to go to Honeycrisp Hill. When did he have time to do all this? I thought we were going to do it together. It was going to be fun.

A voice drifts down the hallway, followed by an old man who appears between two stacks of books.

"Kaliope." He bears a striking resemblance to Dad, though his hair's white and ragged. "Well. Hello. I'm Ian . . . I'm your grandpa." He shoots Dad a look as my eyes nearly bulge from my skull. "You didn't tell her? She looks like a deer in the headlights, Lachlan."

My mouth drops open and the world begins to spin. Who even is this?

My dad never spoke of his father. He was never

around. I'd just imagined Grandma killed him. She's always seemed like the type to kill people.

"Told me *what?*" My voice wobbles.

Ian—my grandpa, I guess—rushes through the boxes and wraps his arms around me in a bearlike hug. He smells like buttery shortbread. "We're going to open a bookstore. Been saving up for it my entire life. Working all over the world, just waiting to retire and reconnect with my family. Gonna have a proper store, and be a proper family."

I glance over his shoulder at Dad. He gives me a cringey grin.

My insides feel like they're boiling and then cooling and then boiling again.

Dad seems to read that on my expression. "I should have told you sooner, I know. But . . . things are going to be different, Kal. Better. You'll see."

"You're retired?" I shift on my feet, trying to sound interested.

"Yep." Ian leans against a box. He frowns. "Worked at the Agency most of my life. They had me traveling all over the world, ran me ragged. I . . . I missed my child's life." His gaze darts to Dad. "But he reached out and . . . gave me a chance."

Did Dad give him a chance so he could pawn me off on his father?

When I was struggling last year, we decided it was time for a change. A big change. Jenny, my therapist, called it anxiety. Sometimes I'm flying high; most times I'm crashing low. We tested meds until we found the right ones, and she told me I'm not alone. But I was. That's why moving to Honeycrisp Hill was supposed to change everything. I'd have magic and community, *and* Dad would be home after school. It was going to be the best thing ever.

But the dream I have of Dad and I eating dinner together and him driving me to the mall dwindles away. Somehow, he'll find a way to go back to working every waking minute, and I'm sure it'll be because of this new "grandpa." Seems like they have a lot in common—they'd rather do anything else than spend time with their kids.

Proper family my butt.

Ian must read my anger, must notice my red face, because he takes a step back. "I can see this is a lot, and I suspect Lachlan wasn't sure I'd even be here today. But I want to be a part of all this. If you'll let me . . ." Now he locks eyes with me.

I glance between Dad and Ian. They both look at me, waiting for an answer. And the way I see it, there's only one thing I can say.

"Okay."

3
Wini

Flour. Sugar. Eggs. Butter. Salt.

Those are the five most important ingredients in a bakery. But here, we have one special addition that makes all the difference: magic. With the right words and a certain level of skill, food enchanters can imbue strong emotions into our food. Not only do our sweets taste amazing, they can change someone's entire perspective, change their day, change their lives. And tonight, the vial of the Jenkinses' love sits in my pocket just waiting to be added into a spell that'll change *everything*.

One drop of true love will act like a sourdough starter in the spell. I'll add it to the recipe, imbue it with flavor, and have a ton of love-inducing product in the end. I'll keep the remaining love in the vial, feeding it little drops here and there, letting it grow. One drop of emotion is nowhere near enough to be useful, and it's *expensive*, which is why the bakery's struggling. But An Enchanted Match spell will create a *lot* of love from a teeny little bit. Free. At least, that's how I'm planning to change

Grandma Bernice's spell. If my idea works, it will revolutionize Wayward Sentiments.

It'll save us.

I thought I'd sneak in after the game, but of course, this kitchen doesn't quit. Aunt Maddie's baking and casting away her troubles and asks me to lend a hand.

My grip tightens on the warped, heavy pan as I tilt it just so over the frothy egg whites, slowly drizzling the hot sugar syrup inside. The mixer shakes the entire table—the movement, much like the mingling scents of cinnamon, chocolate, and honey butter bread, feels like home.

"Slow and steady, Wini," Aunt Maddie says. She slides two yellow cakes from the oven onto the wooden bench. Her apron's dotted with milk chocolate from the caramel pralines she must've made while I was out and that now sit on the counter. My stomach growls at the thought of them, even though that hot chocolate filled my sweets quota for the night. It really is impossible to work around all this delicious food and not be hungry all the time.

"I know, Auntie," I mutter. I want to work on the spell so bad. She's really cramping my style.

If I told her about it, she'd object automatically, even though I'm doing it for all the right reasons. She's opposed to magic that sort of colors outside the lines, she's opposed to "meddling," and even more opposed to magical meddling that colors outside the lines. Her motto: "Mind your business or *I'll* be minding it." And if she found out I did something illegal, I'd rather be thrown in enchanter jail than face her wrath.

Thinking about my crime causes knots in my stomach. I won't—I can't—think about that. No one's gonna find out.

My eyes swivel to the picture above the door. It's Grandma Bernice standing in the center, Wayward Sentiments Café & Sweetery behind her. She's short, with a head of curls tucked beneath a multicolored bandanna. The light bounces off the tiny dark freckles speckled over her brown skin, and she has the widest, most genuine smile fixed on her face.

My gaze narrows on my dad standing beside her. He's goofing for the camera, all toothy grin with his tongue sticking out, his arms wrapped around his mama. He looks so young and free. Not a single line of worry etched into his skin. To the left, Aunt Maddie looks exactly the same as she does now. Same head of voluminous curls, same dark brown skin as Dad.

I like to imagine I look like a cross between Grandma— since I've got these ridiculous (okay, kinda cute) freckles, too—and Aunt Maddie. Truth is, though, I'm the spitting image of my bio mom. Coraline. Her picture is over the fireplace upstairs, out of the public eye.

I know hardly anything about her. I've never even met her.

Grandma would sometimes let little tidbits slip while she was teaching me how to bake as a kid or when I'd help her into bed at night.

Coraline always put too much flour in these cookies. They'd be so tough. Not an enchanter of food and you could tell.

You got that same look Coraline got when she was determined about something.

Apparently Coraline was known for being difficult. *Why, sometimes,* Grandma told me, *people would run down the street when they saw her coming. She was a strong-headed girl. Used to terrify some folks.*

Coraline was Grandma's oldest daughter. She was exiled from Honeycrisp Hill after she cursed the town. Very soon after, she must've met someone and had me. She dropped me off on the bakery doorstep in the dead of summer, birth certificate attached, when I was a little less than two weeks old. No note or special blanket that showed me I was loved. No information about my father.

Not knowing or having her around to answer questions used to bother me. Then, one day, it suddenly stopped mattering to me. I stopped asking questions, stopped wanting to know. Her brother—the one I consider my *real* dad—had been the one to pick up a tiny, wailing thing from the doorstep and raise me.

Dad was in the middle of his four-year pastry degree at the one and only local college when he decided to call me his daughter. He moved back into the family home, continued his education on the weekends, and never looked back. His degree hangs beside the walk-in refrigerator collecting dust. I look at it every time I'm reaching for butter.

Sometimes I'm sure I ruined his life. Especially when I see how time has affected him versus Aunt Maddie. He's never dated, or left home for longer than a few hours here and there. He's been running this bakery with Maddie forever, using up Grandma's savings, and now it's going under.

That's one of the reasons I'm doing this spell. One that'll change everything for the bakery. It'll bring in customers, sure, but most importantly it'll create an emotion without needing to source it from somewhere else. They'll call me a genius; people will flock to our magic. I'll restore the Mosley name. Our bakery will bounce back.

I look down at the mixer, trying not to let the pressure of all that get to me. Inside the bowl are lukewarm egg whites that'll become something extraordinary. They'll become a glossy meringue icing, assuming I don't mess it up. The key—besides the cream of tartar, a pinch of salt, and a clean bowl——is pouring the hot sugar syrup in at the right time. Too soon and it won't whip up firmly, too late and it looks like a gloppy mess. I've been making this soft marshmallow fluff since I could stand on a chair and hover over the mixer, so I know exactly what to look for.

When the egg whites are in a frenzy, growing in size and silkiness like a ballerina's tutu, I set the empty pan aside. My hands drop to the bottom of the metal bowl. The warmth is intense, but not enough to burn me. It needs just a few more minutes with the whisk attachment. I remove my hands and inhale the scent of hot honey rolls cooling on the rack.

Aunt Maddie sets a tray down on the counter and casts a quick sugar spell. *"Crisp this crust without delay, make this sugar into brûlée."* The smell of caramelized sugar permeates the air while Auntie heads to the front of the café. She peeks out, her eyebrows lifted. "Someone bought that store."

I perk up, excitement edging my voice. "The old haunted bookstore?"

"Mm-hm." Maddie takes a sip of tea. I swear she's always drinking the stuff whenever she's about to spill gossip. She's like a walking meme. "I heard it got bought by this guy from up in Boston."

I laugh. *Up in Boston*, like it's so far away. We're only forty-five minutes south.

"You won't believe it, but—"

My dad leans against the doorway that leads to our private courtyard, letting out a long huff. "Why you always telling stories?"

Aunt Maddie spins. "Now listen here, Marcus," she begins, setting her mug down. "I don't got time for you and your negativity today. Honeycrisp Hill is too small to not share the gossip, and these folks 'bout to be our neighbors. Now let me get on with my news." Her lips purse. "They're enchanters."

"So isn't everyone in this town?" Dad tilts his head to the side to consider. "Wait, they're not food enchanters, right? We already got Russell with his magical pizza, and the Yangs with their . . ." He sucks in his lips as if salivating. "Delicious restaurant. Goodness, I wish we could afford takeout from there right now . . . Anyway, we don't need any more competition."

"For real," Aunt Maddie agrees. "They'll be selling books, but . . ."

She doesn't finish as we peek through the window. Our eyes take in the teeny light flickering in the bookshop window. What she doesn't say is that they could sell delightful pastries and coffees with those books. And that'd be the last nail in our coffin.

Honeycrisp Hill is a haven for enchanters. Everyone in town has magic. We have a monthly town hall meeting, but it's mostly ridiculous and nothing ever gets done besides people pointing fingers at one another or community problem-solving on spells that backfire. And we never talk about the curse or how to drum up tourism. People can come in just fine, but inhabitants who were here when the curse was cast can't leave unless they want to be regular magicless humans. Unsurprisingly, no one has left.

"Maybe you and Dad should—" I stop when the door jingles. "Aren't we closed?"

"Five minutes till eight," Dad says. "Want to go handle that? I'm not dressed."

I untie the straps of my black-and-white polka-dot apron, place it beside the radio by the door, and shimmy past Aunt Maddie into the dining area. The decor's a combo of old and whimsical. Fake tree branches hang from the ceiling covered in twinkling fairy lights, while fake pumpkins sit atop the four wrought iron tables, little battery-operated candles flickering inside. Garlands of autumn leaves dangle around, giving ultimate fall vibes. We're sticklers for keeping up the seasonal atmosphere, even though we're often the only ones to see it.

The display cases lining the walls are nearly empty. We stopped making Envy Brownies, Fussy Focaccia,

Carefree Lemon Curd Cupcakes, and Stormy Scallion Scones since the demand is so low. We only have a smattering of products like Brave Butterscotch Bonnets and Calming Croissants.

Before I can get my gloves on, a tall man in a disheveled but expensive business suit stalks up to the counter across the shiny red-and-white checkered floors, eyes darting around the shelves.

"How can I help you today?" My voice is saccharine sweet, just like the goodies that used to be overflowing from trays around me.

He clears his throat, running his hand through his perfect hair. "I'm looking for"—his voice falls to a whisper—"Energizing Eclairs?"

I smile before sliding across the counter to a glass box at the end. Golden brown eclairs gently tumble from a woven basket Grandma Bernice made in the fifties but looks very niche and artisan. My style. The fairy lights hit the chocolate coating just right. Picture perfect. We only have four left.

"How many would you like?"

He adjusts his tie. "All of them. Do you have more in the back?"

My eyebrows lift. Not that we don't need the cash, but this could be dangerous. "Even eating one of these will have you going anywhere from thirty-six to forty-eight hours."

"They're for the staff." He rubs the exhaustion from his eyes. "All hands on deck."

I take in his suit again before meeting his deep brown eyes. I'm not supposed to do this, but I can tell when someone's in need. "I'll grab the rest in the back."

The corners of his lips lift. "Please."

I dart back into the walk-in to grab the extra eclairs. I package them up quickly, closing the flaps with our logo sticker, and push the box across the counter to him. "That'll be—"

He hands me five hundred dollars before I can even finish. "If they're as good as I've been told, they're worth more than this."

My eyes feel like they're bulging out of my head. He takes the box with a tiny grin.

"Please take a card. C-come back," I stutter. He grabs one from beside the register before leaving the shop.

Maddie appears beside me, her jaw dropped. "Wow."

"Dad!" I scream. "Dad, he gave us five hundred bucks!"

Don't do the happy dance. Don't do your happy dance, I tell myself as my body begins to vibrate and my arms swing into my usual happy dance. Well, at least I tried.

My dad laughs from the doorway, hands full of mail. "Big seller. If we could count on sales like that, we wouldn't have to close, huh?"

"And then one day I'll run this place." I give him my

most dazzling smile. And then it falls. "Wait—close? We're . . . officially closing?"

He clears his throat, his eyes flickering quickly to Maddie. My stomach tightens. "Ah—no. Maybe. Just . . . you know what I mean." He waves the handful of bills at me, but all I can see are numbers with minus signs and *overdue* in bold red font.

Panic starts to grip me. Big sale aside, the ingredients we have to source, like Confidence and Bravery, have tripled in cost in the past couple years. None more so than happiness, which already costs a small fortune for a single vial. Without it in stock, it's only a matter of time till production stops.

I can't tell how he feels about it, we don't usually talk about our failures. But if this spell works . . . I *know* I can use the foundation to create more spells. Source *more* emotion for free.

I have to do this spell. *Tonight.*

Dad begins to head back into the kitchen. I cut him off, a plan forming in my head fast. "You and Aunt Maddie should go talk to Russell. You know, just to make sure that the new enchanters haven't applied for a food license. That's the last thing we need."

Aunt Maddie frowns, and Dad scrubs his chin. *Say yes.* I need some alone time to do my spell.

"We can't deal with any competition. We're barely

making ends meet already . . ." Maddie scrunches her lips together.

"You're right about that." Dad glances at the clock on the wall. "Russell's shouldn't be at peak capacity right now. We might be able to catch him before he's slammed."

Aunt Maddie takes off her apron and they stride past me, already talking between them about what they should say. I let myself fade into nothingness, hoping they forget I'm here. As the door opens, I whisper a spell under my breath.

"Keys to open the door, keys to lock it, move the keys from his coat to my pocket." It's not a standard spell, but the keys weigh down my apron pocket just the same. I smile to myself.

After they're out, I run to the store window, put up the closed sign, and lock the door. I rush through, turning off the main lights, and scurry back into the kitchen. Behind the rolling cart of flour lies the book and a small box of the ingredients I've been collecting. My movements are frantic. Time's already running out and any moment they could be back. The pizzeria's only next door, and Russell's not normally a chatty dude. *Hurry up.*

I plop the ingredients onto the counter and open the box. Inside are four items that took time to gather. First, Dad's favorite vinyl: Stevie Wonder's *The Definitive*

Collection (which is also my favorite). Next—and this is the part I added to tweak the recipe—his favorite pastry: a slice of blueberry muffin bread I made just this morning before school. Then there's a very teeny lock of his hair, which was the hardest item to procure since he's been shaving it off regularly for ten years. Collecting it from the sink wasn't fun. Lastly, I have a small scrap of paper describing the perfect man my dad is looking for.

1. *Must love to dance (oldies, especially)*
2. *Has to love desserts and good food in general*
3. *Favorite holiday should be Halloween*
4. *Loves goofballs, especially Winifred (Dad's the best.)*
5. *Likes watching black-and-white movies*
6. *Will never hurt us, abandon us, or betray our trust*

Dad told me that last one once when I was a kid, and I haven't forgotten. I set the vial of sparkly love beside everything else.

I have to focus on creating love for a person in order to create the love in the spell. Makes sense; love is a human emotion, so it has to come from some kind of actual human connection. And I figured, why not start with Dad? I'm not ready for a relationship, and Aunt Maddie would kill me if I messed with her. So, Dad it is.

The spell requires me to place everything together,

whisper the ancient words, and then . . . something will happen. I imagine it'll work like my usual food magic—the spell will absorb into the blueberry bread. From there, all I have to do is get Dad to eat it, and then he'll feel super ready to fall in love. I'll do a spell to extract the emotion and then I'll have plenty of love to put into sweets. From there, I'll find a way to tweak the recipe to create other emotions to extract. It's very clever.

With a little more energy than necessary, I throw open Grandma Bernice's book to the page I bookmarked. The Mosley family grimoire is somewhere upstairs, but this one is Grandma's personal journal of spells she was working on. *An Enchanted Match*, it reads, with a warning in parenthesis: (*Doesn't work.*).

Well, I'm going to *make* it work. I'm determined to save the bakery, and if anyone in this family can do it, it's me. I don't quit.

Take each personal item and stack atop one another. Wrap the hair around it and tie tight.

Well, that's impossible. I'll just use kitchen twine—goodness knows we have that somewhere around here. I open drawers and shove them shut frantically. It's gotta be here . . .

The door jiggles, and a voice bounces off the glass. "Wini, you there? I forgot my keys." Dad taps on the window. I grimace. Time's running out!

I ignore him, finding the twine behind the radio. I tie it around the four items and read the last line.

Top with one drop of true love.

I unscrew the vial and quickly tip it.

The door rattles again. "Wini!"

Repeat these words: Heart and soul, body and mind, the perfect match you must find. Follow the list. Know thy spell. Imbue the sweet where we dwell—and then the part I added: *Work thine magic, from above and below, from wary hope bring them love and GROW.*

The words leave my lips in a flurry and for a second, I worry nothing will happen. And then, just as that worry turns to panic and the doorknob twists open, the lights flicker once before plunging me into near darkness. Only the vial with love inside pulses with a faint, purplish glow.

I let out a startled choke and then remember my dad is coming and he can't see what I've done. My fingers graze the countertop, finding the edge of the book first, and I stick it behind the flour cart once more. Then I go back for the blueberry bread . . . only to find nothing. Nothing at all. Surely it can't have just disappeared?

I pocket the vial before bolting toward the stairs as if I'm coming down, then open the door for my grumbling dad.

"Well that's weird," I say into the darkness. "I was

about to—" Lie. I need a lie. But what'll do here? Dad's especially talented at knowing when I'm lying. "Make some tea before, you know, coming back down to clean up, when the lights went out."

"Mm. I'm surprised they haven't come back on. We have a backup generator," he says somewhere near the wooden bench where I was just standing.

Where the actual heck did the bread go? How is he going to eat it and be overcome with love enough that I can extract it?

"Um . . ." Thankfully I'm relieved from having to come up with something to say when the lights blink back on as if nothing happened. Aunt Maddie comes through the door, carrying a box of pizza, and I act surprised, hoping Dad's gaze doesn't linger too long on me.

"You okay, Wini? You look like you saw a sign for a sale at the thrift store." He smiles like someone who doesn't know his daughter just tried to do a powerful spell that'll mess with his life and failed massively.

"Yeah, I'm fine." My stomach's in knots. "What did Russell say?"

Aunt Maddie slides the pizza onto the table. "He said as far as he knows, they just plan on selling books. Then he gave us a free pie with all our favorite toppings—can you believe it? Russell is the cheapest man alive."

"He likes you." I try to calm my pounding heart by directing attention elsewhere. I'm so mad I just want to knead bread dough into a floury mess. I can't believe I failed.

"I'm not interested. First of all—" Her finger comes up to keep count. Her rants always involve a list of grievances. "Remember when he told me I looked like a discount Beyoncé?"

"We were teenagers, Maddie," my dad interjects.

Her eyebrows rise, and she juts her jaw out. "I don't care. You don't say that to anyone. Even if you think it's a compliment. Second of all, he used up the last of the hot fudge at the town ice cream social last year. That was just rude and selfish. You know the hot fudge makes Tina's ice cream bearable."

Dad opens his mouth to say something and then shuts it automatically. He can't win this fight. Tina, the town selectwoman, makes large vats of ice cream for the annual town social every first of July. Her ice cream isn't the worst . . . only it tastes like nothing. Like eating a cold cloud. Although clouds probably have more flavor.

"And third of all," she continues, "he asked me on a date by saying, and I quote, 'You ain't getting any younger or cuter, so why not go out with me?' Dear lord, I almost hit that man straight in the jaw."

Dad and I nod as if this is the first time we've heard this story.

"Okay, so Russell's the worst. He's dead to all of us," Dad says. "But does that mean we can't enjoy the pizza?"

Aunt Maddie smiles, rant forgotten. "I say we do a quick cleanup and watch a movie tonight while we eat it. Whaddya say?"

Dad nudges in beside me. "Sounds good. We should watch *Meet Me in St. Louis*. I love that one."

"Ugh." Aunt Maddie gives a small shake of her head. "You always wanna watch that. But okay."

A sudden wind howls outside, rattling the windows and crashing open the bakery door. Scattering leaves fly by in shades of brilliant red and orange.

"That must have been what knocked the lights out. Weird weather," Dad says.

I can't help but feel he's wrong. Outside the streetlamps flicker, casting shadows on the building walls in the form of something . . . someone. They stand there in a long black cloak and a strangely pointy hat. The shadow slithers closer, becoming more defined and real, and I yelp. Because in that impossible shadow, my name appears. *Winifred.*

Then it disappears. My mouth flops open and my heart races.

"Did you . . . ?" I ask Maddie as Dad bolts the door shut.

"Did I . . . what?" she asks, brows lifted. There's no panic in her tone or features. She's as casual as always.

She must not have seen it. Or it must not have been there.

"Never mind," I say, shaking my head.

It couldn't have been real. My mind's just playing tricks on me.

And yet I can't seem to shake the feeling that something—or some*one*—is coming.

4
Kal

Early Friday morning, the car's packed up and we're ready to go.

Ian tried to talk to me, but I've given him the coldest of shoulders. I don't know him and I don't want him to feel welcome. This was supposed to be an adventure for Dad and me—I don't see how he's going to fit in and I don't plan on letting him. I get into the passenger seat, leaving Ian to scrunch into the back among all the boxes.

After only twenty minutes, Dad gets the idea to stop at a diner, the Brookston Inn, for cake and coffee. Ian—Grandpa? I haven't decided what to call him yet—hasn't said a word. He's mostly stoic. In his own mind. Staring out the window. Every once in a while, during music breaks, I think I hear him mumbling in another language under his breath.

I'd ask, but he doesn't seem like he's in the mood for talking. And I'm not entirely sure I care.

"We're only another twenty minutes away," I mutter as Dad pulls over at the inn by the side of the road. The parking lot is deserted. The building has gray and brown streaks on the outside, and the windows are blacked out.

Not the kind of place where I'd want to eat.

"Dad, it's closed."

Dad gives me the Look. "Do you see a closed sign?"

I let a long exhale loose. "No, but—"

"No buts, come on. You too, old man." He climbs out of the car and takes a big whiff of air like he's been driving for hours.

Ian perks up as we undo our seat belts. Dad's already walking toward the building. I get out, Ian following. I toss a scowl at him over my shoulder but he doesn't seem to notice or care.

We go up the rickety stairs, treading gingerly. The last thing I want is to fall through some icky wood on the side of the road and get splinters. I cringe thinking of it.

"C'mon." Dad holds the door open for us. A little bell jingles, alerting the ghosts likely waiting inside. I grimace as dust kicks up under my Vans. Dad can't be serious. Then he starts talking slowly and carefully.

"*Lachlan stood with his family in the run-down hallway. Suddenly, the magic revealed itself to them . . .*"

When he's done, everything around us changes.

Sound comes through the teeny hallway, conversations and laughter. And there are mouth-watering scents drifting toward me. Citrus and cinnamon. Something peachy.

"Ah good, enchanted," Ian says, striding past me before rounding a corner and disappearing.

"What is this?" My eyes widen as sconces flicker on beside my head. Old-timey music trickles into my ears as if we're in a black-and-white movie and colors have begun to appear.

"This is enchantment," Dad says, taking my hand. "Enchanters have to conceal their magic outside of Honeycrisp Hill so non-magic people don't stumble into our world. We use *our* magic to unlock it. It's how we've existed over the centuries." The ground beneath me is somehow less rickety than before and much less dusty. Suddenly my dingy Vans feel out of place.

Once deeper into the strange nothingness, my mind's blown. I can't move while I take in every detail. Glowing, glittery orbs hover above us, someone's playing a piano somewhere, and there's a wooden bar directly in front, packed with people.

Windows I hadn't seen from the outside are open, but the views are all different. One shows a garden full of luscious hues of green and patches of vibrant flowers shimmering in the perfect sunlight, while another less than a foot away shows a crowded city street in downpouring rain. The last one, unobscured by anyone sitting at the table, displays stars. Millions and millions of stars.

The only word I can think of falls from my lips. "Dad."

He drops my hand and wraps his arm around my shoulder. "It's a lot to take in, I know. But you'll get the hang of it."

Just as my eyes adjust to all the colors, the magic, the everything-ness happening all around me, Ian barges into view. I throw another scowl in his direction.

"Got us a table, c'mon."

Dad pulls me forward as my head swings between people who barely turn to regard us. Some are covered in tattoos and piercings, some look like they're well into their sixties and enjoy drinking tea in the English countryside with their starched cardigans and cat-eye glasses. Others have wild hair colors, and others look no different from me. Just normal. Boring.

In the far back, there's a woman with brown hair, dressed in all black with matching lipstick. Our eyes lock before her gaze flicks to Ian. Beyond her, the room keeps changing. Nothing matches. Tables pop up from nowhere, all in different styles. Ours is covered in a lacy white tablecloth, with a vase of bright yellow sunflowers.

I perch on an emerald velvet cushion attached to the kind of old, high-backed chair I've never seen outside of movies. My mouth is still open.

"I see your style hasn't changed so much," Dad says to Ian. "You've always loved your afternoon tea. Wonder if you'll pinch my fingers if I put just a bit too much sugar in."

My brows raise, temporarily distracted from this strange, new world I've found myself in. He sounds bitter. Angry, almost. My dad's temperament is usually so agreeable, if a bit impatient. I realize then that maybe Dad doesn't want Ian here, either. Which begs the question, why *is* he here?

"Let it go, Lachlan. You promised." Ian's voice is heavy, and I wonder what else happened between them. "I've only been retired a few weeks. We can't move forward if you keep making me pay for the past."

An uncomfortable silence falls between us. I tap my fingers against the table. This is supposed to be a fresh start but so far, it's already being overshadowed. Ian is ruining this for everyone. Dad inhales sharply, ready to snap, and the last thing I want is having my first magical experience tainted.

"We should order high tea," I suggest, pointing to the menu written in chalk beside a gilded mirror. "It comes with cakes, something called sarnies—"

"Sandwiches," Dad says, nudging me with his elbow. "Like cucumber and sausage rolls."

"Mmm, that sounds good." My voice is a few octaves

too high, but I push on. "And you get a whole pot of tea. Everyone will be happy." Dad ignores the awkwardness in my tone, giving me a full-wattage grin. I find myself returning it, really trying to make the best of a weird situation.

"Haven't had high tea in a long time," Ian replies, splaying his hands on the table and making eye contact with a waitress. "Not since you were a kid."

The waitress brings over a large three-tiered stand and sets it in the center of the table. Three teapots material-ize. She sets down dainty cups and saucers and is about to leave when my brows knit together as I realize what just happened. "But are you going to take our order? How do you know what kind of tea we want?"

Her hair's a vibrant purple that matches the floral pattern on her dress. When she speaks, her accent, something European, is slight. "*I* don't, but the tea-pot does. These"—her arms wave around—"are all enchanted. Please enjoy and call if you need any-thing." She offers me a friendly nod and then maneu-vers between the tables.

My dad's fingers touch the edge of my hand. "I know it's a lot, but you're going to learn, and I'm going to be here for you. No more overworking and late nights. Okay?"

His green eyes flash, and I see guilt in them. My hand

bumps against his briefly before pulling away. I really hope he means it. I'm so tired of being alone, of gray days and trying to be positive, putting on a smile and being weird just to cover it all up.

"What kind do you have?" I'm trying. I guess.

"Blueberry muffin," Dad answers, dropping a lump of brown sugar into his cup before pouring in the tea. The sugar dissolves instantly. "My favorite."

The scent wafts toward me. It's amazing how much it smells like fresh blueberry muffins straight from the oven. "Can I try?"

My dad slides a cup over to me, as Ian clears his throat.

"I used to make blueberry muffins for Lachlan all the time," Ian says. "It was my way of dealing with stress. Your grandmother . . ." He doesn't finish that line of thought. "It was our special thing. Every Sunday."

Ian glances at Dad, but Dad's staring at the window full of stars, tense. Ian sighs, placing his hand on the table in front of Dad. "Lachlan, I—"

"Well, if it isn't Ian Clarke." The woman who was sitting in the back suddenly stands in front of our table, her black-lined lips drawn into a tight smile. "Funny seeing you here just as wicked magic has been summoned to Honeycrisp Hill."

The three of us sit in silence and I'm not sure if I should continue drinking my tea. She regards Dad and me slowly before returning her glare to Ian. He glares right back.

"I have no idea what you're talking about," he says stiffly.

She makes a noise in her throat. "I'll be watching you, Mr. Clarke. There are no such things as coincidences." And with that, she stalks off with one last, pointed look at each of us.

"Who was that?" I ask.

"Enchantment Agency," Ian answers. I can tell that's all he's going to say.

Dad's not satisfied with that answer, though. "I've invited you here to be a part of our family, to share our time together, but you have *yet* to tell me what happened and what it had to do with the Enchantment Agency. Why would they still be watching you? I thought you retired."

I try to melt into my seat with the rim of the cup pressed to my lips.

Ian shakes his head. "You don't want to know."

"For once in your life, just talk about it!" Dad slams his hand on the table, rattling the saucers. The clinking of porcelain turns heads toward us. My dad, the man who is almost never angry, is making a scene. A big, ugly scene. "You left me twenty years ago for your job. Not a word. Not even a single call or letter. Nothing. We never knew where you were, if you were in danger or hurt. You were always more loyal to the Agency than to us. And now they're watching you?"

The chair scrapes against the wooden floor as Ian pushes himself to his feet. "I'll go wait in the car."

He weaves through the room, leaving Dad's face a bright, enraged red. He shoves a cucumber sandwich in his mouth, either his way of not talking to me about what happened or stress-eating.

"Dad . . ."

"Not now, Kal." His tone is pleading. "I don't want to talk about it."

"Look, I know we . . . things are . . . whatever between us. But I'm here, you know. I'm a good listener." I cough before taking a scone dotted with dried fruit and the little bowl of clotted cream. I've never had either before, but I don't want to waste food. This isn't one of those movies where everyone sits down to eat something amazing and then no one eats because of emotions. Amazingly, I'm not the emotional one today. What a change of pace.

Dad turns to me. "Kal . . ." His head drops. "I'll never do to you what he did to me. I'm sorry for not spending more time with you. For not . . ." He doesn't finish the sentence.

Tears suddenly prick at my eyes, and I sniff once.

"Yeah, okay." I clear my throat. "So why is Ian here? Why did you invite him?" I didn't mean for it to come out so sharp, but it does. This was supposed to be a fresh start . . . for *me*. "Is it because of what my therapist said?"

"No." My dad stares deeply into my eyes, and I attempt to look anywhere else. "He reached out to me a few months ago saying he was done, that he didn't want to be an agent anymore. We talked about what we both wanted to do—how I didn't want to be a journalist anymore. I wasn't sure what would happen. Then one thing led to another. He was trying so hard and I thought . . . We can't always do everything alone, Kal. And my— Ian, he needs family, too. But mostly, it's because with him running the store with me, I'll have more time. I want to be the father I didn't have for a daughter who has always deserved better."

"Okay." I sniff again. I want to believe him, but my heart is cautious. Protective. I've been let down too many times. "You have to promise me: No more lies or last-minute jobs."

"I promise." He drops a hand to wipe away his own tears. I guess everyone in this family is emotional.

I take a sausage roll and pop it in my mouth. Dad pours himself a cup of tea and smiles. A fresh start. Magic.

I lower my voice as to not draw further attention. "Dad, what's the Enchantment Agency?"

He exhales slowly. "The Enchantment Agency regulates magic, like officers of the law." When he sees my face twist, trying to understand why they'd be watching Ian, he waves a hand. "Don't worry about all that. It's not our business. Besides, I want you to try something." He takes the small notebook from his pocket. Attached on the side is his favorite fountain pen, and he hands both to me. "I want you to write three sentences about this table we're sitting at, but change one thing about each. Okay?"

For a moment, my breath lodges in my throat. "You're really going to let me do this?"

Dad grins. "Better late than never, right?"

My nerves roil in my gut, but I take the notebook from him, my thoughts about enchantment law enforcement and Ian fleeing my mind. With a quick click of the pen, I press the tip down and write whatever comes to mind first.

The white tablecloth is now a midnight blue, pocked with sparkly silver stars. The teacup is now a champagne flute. And . . .

And . . .

What else can I change?

The blueberry muffin tea is now a blueberry muffin.

I set the pen down.

"Now I want you to say these words: *'By my hand these words were writ, by my magic they will transmit, weave reality should you grant, with my voice I do enchant.'* Then read your sentences."

I stare at him, my heart pounding. A real spell. "What if nothing happens?"

"It's close to Samhain, All Hallows' Eve . . ." He smirks as I shoot him a glare. "Halloween. Our magic is at its strongest right now. What I'm saying is there's no way you can go wrong. It's basic word enchantment, and you're a Clarke. We're powerful."

My legs shake under the table as I swallow my nerves. "By my hand these words were writ, by my magic they will transmit, weave reality should you grant, with my voice I do enchant . . ." The words fly off my tongue and there's a surge of something within me. Something warm and *right*. I say my written sentences and then wait.

Seconds pass.

My voice cracks a little. "Did I do it right?"

"Let's see," Dad says.

The teacup is still a teacup. The tablecloth is still white. But then he lifts the pot of the tea, and inside, there's a warm blueberry muffin as if it were baked within. I gasp.

I run my fingers over the tablecloth. "Why didn't it all work?"

My dad takes a bite of the blueberry muffin. "Your first spell wasn't going to be perfect. But I'd say that was successful, wouldn't you?"

I take a bite of blueberry muffin. It's warm and sweet, crumbly, and tastes just right. My brain feels like it might explode. I did it. "I guess so."

"You'll get your magic learner's permit first day of enchantment school so you can begin doing Level One spells on your own, but I think you'll be ready." Dad scoops up another bite. "This is actually really, really good." He scoops up another big bite. "How do you feel?"

A smile pulls at my cheeks. I don't care that it wasn't an absolute success. No, I can't care about the tablecloth or the teacup because I finally got my chance. The muffin worked. And my words finally matter.

I can't wait to do more. *Be* more. "Powerful."

Dad's lips curve at the corners until his eyes glaze over distractedly. "Do you hear Stevie Wonder or is it just me?"

I pause, drowning out the conversations and clinks of teacups around us. And there, so gently my ears can only pick up on a few soft bars, is Stevie Wonder's voice. I look around but no one else seems to hear it, or maybe they're all too busy enjoying their tea to notice. I shrug as Dad's nose crinkles and he sings about everything being all right and out of sight. I smile, happiness spreading through me for the first time in a long time.

I am powerful, and things are going to change.

5

Wini

There's a commotion at the bookstore. The new family is moving in.

I'm sure all of Main Street is watching right now, wondering how long it'll be before they move out again, what with it being haunted and all. Maybe I shouldn't call it haunted. At least not until I've actually seen a ghost.

The sky crackles overhead, and I look up. The weather's been unusually stormy since . . . well, since I cast the spell. But I haven't seen the shadow figure again. Nothing weird has happened. So it must all be in my imagination, right? It didn't work, and that's that.

I peer out the window as an older man with long white hair carries boxes into the store. There's a younger man, too, and a girl, who's about my height and wearing a funky hat. They stand, smiling at the storefront with boxes in their arms. They look nice. Happy. Friendly, even.

The girl turns to glare in my direction—did she see me staring like a weirdo? I duck down.

Should I introduce myself? Immediately, I feel my throat tighten, thinking of the rejection, but . . . she knows nothing about me. She knows absolutely nothing about my family name and the drama connected to it.

She has no reason to automatically dislike me.

The thought fills me with something warm. Maybe . . . hope?

If I can talk to her first, before the other kids at school, maybe . . . maybe she'll want to be my friend.

I quickly take off my apron and open up a box to shove some goodies inside. Aunt Maddie says people tend to like you more when you give them sweets. So I box up some cinnamon croissants, cheesy gougères fresh from the oven meant for our dinner tonight, hot fudge brownies, some of those caramel pralines from yesterday, garlic and herb focaccia with salty butter and spicy tomato confit (a fancier version of jam), and my personal recipe, Honeycrisp Hill shortbread that tastes especially nice with a cup of blackberry tea. I toss in a few bags of tea as well.

Right. There's that. Now the hard part.

"Hi, I'm Wini Mosley, and I'm your neighbor. I've brought you treats. Be my friend, please!" I say aloud with conviction. Seems simple enough. Too desperate?

With a deep breath, shoulders back, and all the

confidence I can muster, I open the bakery door and step out. The rain has let up to a light mist, but how long it'll stay that way is anyone's guess. The family has stopped moving boxes inside, probably because of the storm.

The leaves scattered on the ground stick to my boots as I trudge a few feet down Main Street. I stop outside the store as rain drizzles along the window. I probably look like a creep standing here without an umbrella, holding a box of pastries and tea, staring at a family unpack boxes of books.

A sudden breeze nips at my cheeks and I turn briefly in the direction of the Adachi estate on the far end of the street, surrounded by woods. The Adachi estate is known for its magic. Rumor has it that generations ago when Maricel Adachi moved here from the Philippines with her husband, they were so powerful that they transformed their land with magic. Their power lingers in the soil, lives within the roots of the trees, blooms like the flowers, and climbs like the ivy. It's even said that their home is a heart, and magic pumps through the walls. But outside, it surrounds you, makes you feel strong.

Every single descendent is buried on the land to amplify that power. Magic flocks there, flourishes, and thrives. If you want to do a spell that's complicated and needs an extra push, you come to these woods.

If you're brave enough.

A chill coming from those woods and whipping down Main Street seems ominous, but I don't have time to think about that.

I knock on the door and wave at the older man, who strides toward it. He's tall, draped in a baggy, button-down shirt, khaki slacks that are at least two sizes too big and yet seem to match his unbrushed, shaggy hair.

He opens it only a crack, causing me to move back a little. "Sorry, we aren't open yet." His accent's cool, different. "Planning on Halloween, make a big to-do of it. See you then—"

"Yeah, hi, sorry," I cut him off. "I'm your neighbor. My family owns that bakery back there. I wanted to introduce . . . um . . . myself." I plaster a big smile on my face. "I brought snacks?"

The older man seems to understand, as he steps aside and swings the door open for me.

"Oh yes, a neighbor. Hello. Please come in, and excuse the boxes," he says. He points to the other two who have their backs to us, bickering about who has to get the ladder in the basement. "My name's Ian. That's my son, Lachlan, and his daughter, Kaliope—Kal."

I nod, waiting for them to turn, but they don't. Ian coughs pointedly to get their attention.

Lachlan pushes back the thick black hair that falls

across his forehead and stands straighter. He's tall and sturdy like his father and wears a crisp blue button-down shirt with a matching cardigan, round black glasses, and fitted jeans. "Oh, hello."

"Hi," the girl named Kal says, her cheeks a bit pink. Her flowy brown hair escapes a black porkpie hat as she clutches a few books to her chest. She's got on ripped jeans, a leather jacket, and chunky boots. One of the shoelaces dangles dangerously close to the ground. She's cute, like in a punk Disney princess kind of way.

"So, what are you?" I ask, and immediately regret it. Her mouth contorts and her eyes narrow. I should've asked that in a different way. "I'm sorry, I meant, enchanters? I mean what kind of enchanters, not . . . um . . . the other thing. It's really rude to ask where people are from by being like, oh what are you, as if you aren't, you know, human . . . ?"

Lachlan chuckles and shoots Kal a grin. "We're word enchanters." He gestures around to all the boxes packed with books. "We're soon-to-be booksellers, too."

Before I can say that's cool, Kal rolls her eyes.

"*They're* word enchanters; I'm still figuring my magic out. I'm a beginner." Kal grimaces and shifts on her feet. "What kind of enchanter are you?"

I hold up the box and a rush of pride heats my cheeks.

"Food enchanter. We own the bakery, Wayward Sentiments, just across the street. We're really good at what we do."

Kaliope nods, hands fidgeting a bit by her sides. "I actually did a bit of food enchanting yesterday, I think. It was my first spell but the food part was the easiest."

"Food enchanting's not easy. It requires skill." My brow furrows and my grip tightens on the sweets. "I've been doing it my whole life and there are still spells I can't do."

She shakes her head. "I didn't mean that it was easy, I mean . . ." Her voice trails off when there's a knock on the door. We both make eye contact and then turn toward the sound. Not gonna lie, I'm not a fan of this Kaliope girl. I think I'd better get out of here before I say something just as mean.

Ian excuses himself and rushes to answer. "Oh, hello there. You must be—"

And in steps Dad. He must have seen me walking here on his way home from . . . wherever. Recently, he's been distant, always leaving to run mysterious errands around town. I think it has something to do with the bakery's bills, but he'd never tell me that.

He gives me a look as water pools around his feet, as if he's been standing in the rain for a long time. Lachlan strides forward, handing him a small towel he took from behind a box-covered counter with a smile. "Hi."

Dad stiffens, taking the towel, and gurgles something that may be hello. In the background, Stevie Wonder's "I Wish" plays softly. They exchange a very long, almost too long, smile while Kaliope and I stand there, avoiding each other.

"We should be going. The bakery can't run itself," I say with a small, fake laugh. I gently nudge Dad back toward the door.

"So you run the bakery, too." Lachlan's gaze still hasn't left Dad. "It's the family business, right? This is our first family business. Any . . . um . . . tips for success?"

Dad steps closer, shutting me and Kal out. "Well, we aren't exactly doing our best now, but if I had some tips, it would be to make sure you have a good treasury enchanter. Wally's office is two buildings down. The man can do anything with numbers; taking his advice is probably how our business survived as long as it has."

Lachlan nods, very seriously. "Treasury enchanter . . . Wow, I've been so far away from enchanting, I've forgotten how many specialties there are." Kal's lips twitch at that, and I'd feel bad for her since she said she was a beginner, but she also kind of insulted me, so . . . "When we're all settled in, would you like to come to dinner? It'll give me the chance to crack open my favorite cookbooks.

Oh, we can make it Halloween themed. Halloween is my favorite."

"Mine too! I'd like that!" Dad nearly shouts and then, seeming to remember the rest of us, amends, "*We* would love that. Or you can come by the . . ." He trails off suddenly. "I love this song. Are you a big Stevie Wonder fan?"

"What song?" Ian pokes his head up from a box. "I can't find the radio—"

"I do love Stevie Wonder," Lachlan says, ignoring his father. "I think I have a copy of his greatest hits around here somewhere."

They continue talking about music while Kal looks bored, drumming her fingers against her thigh. I've got a lot going on in my head. *Has to love desserts and good food in general . . . Favorite holiday should be Halloween.*

What if . . .

No. But . . .

Maybe . . . An Enchanted Match . . . worked somehow?

I mean, loads of people listen to Stevie Wonder. But how many of them have sparkles in their eyes like Lachlan does for Dad? But that can't be right, because the spell didn't leave the blueberry muffin bread behind for me to use. It didn't create a potion for love, so . . . what *did* it do?

Ian grumbles and his eyes widen at something in the window behind us. The atmosphere changes so quickly that we swivel to look as a woman in a long black dress with a tight bun atop her head and piercing green eyes scans us. Nerves flutter in the pit of my stomach.

Something about her gaze gives me goose bumps. I rub my arm nervously. "Do you know her?" We know everyone in this town. Maybe she's with them?

"The lady from the Enchantment Agency," Kal answers. "She said she was here investigating"—her eyes dart to Ian—"uh, a wickedness that's been called to town?"

My blood runs cold. A wickedness was called to the town? What kind of wickedness?

Loads of thoughts swim in my head. What if it was An Enchanted Match? That's not really possible, right? I mean, a love spell can't call a wickedness, right? Right. But then almost immediately after, there was that shadowy figure on the street saying *my name*. The stormy weather began. The stormy weather that's still happening now. And the muffin bread did go missing.

Oh no. No no no . . .

The Enchantment Agency might be here for *me*. I could be in big, big trouble. It's bad enough I stole love for the spell. Calling a wickedness to town—the shadow? That's super bad. And what if it's an evil creature, like a witch? The last witch in our town—my *mom*—cast a curse and someone died.

What if they track the spell back to me? Can they do that? If they can, they'll put me in jail—worse, strip me of my magic entirely. Permanently.

I'd be just like my mom. Everyone in town would say they always knew I'd go bad.

As the woman walks out of sight down the street, stopping to talk to neighbors, the conversation resumes as if everything's completely normal. My heart is pounding in my ears and I can't really hear what anyone says over it.

There's laughter and questions about the sweets I stuffed into the box. Looks shared between Lachlan and my dad. Ian shifts some books from the counter. There's a mention of school and Kal.

But all I can think about is running out of here.

If I don't stop An Enchanted Match, I may have ruined not only my future, but the entire town. And losing the bakery would be the least of our problems.

6

Kal

There's muffled whispering coming from a box of books in the corner. I bet they're enchanted. To be fair, nearly all the books we've been moving in are enchanted—that's what we'll be selling after all—but these ones are in a box marked *Ian's—DO NOT TOUCH.*

We've been moving stuff into the store and upstairs for several hours and I could be hallucinating from hunger. The high tea was forever ago, and although we still have sweets left in the box from Wini and her dad, my stomach's rumbling for something more substantial.

"You are no queen. You are a petulant child who knows no such thing as the truly wicked," one voice says.

"How dare you!" the other objects. *"Do you expect me to be wounded by some green creature with an aversion to water? What a farce!"*

"No, I expect you to respect your superiors, dear, by closing your obnoxiously dull mouth."

The ancient clock chimes, tugging at my attention. It's eight p.m., which coincides with the rumbling in my stomach. I tune out the voices.

"Dad. Food?"

My dad's voice comes from somewhere behind a mountain of boxes. "There's Russell's Pizza across the street. Want to head over there in twenty?"

"Sure," I say. Ian's arm pops through a gap of cardboard before the rest of him appears. "Do you hear that arguing or am I just tired?"

He chuckles. "It's the Queen of Hearts from *Alice in Wonderland* and the Wicked Witch from *The Wizard of Oz*. No idea which one, better not to ask." He stands up, hovering over me slightly. "They'll be upstairs in our personal library."

That's weird. I thought they were just fictional characters, not actual people living inside a book. But then, I don't know much about the enchanting world. Which I don't want to admit to or talk about with Ian. "Why do you have them?"

"Sometimes, the best place for evil enchanted books is far from magicless people, tucked away on a shelf, guarded by word enchanters." He regards me carefully, leaning against the pile of boxes. "You have to understand that you are a Clarke. Our words have power. Which is why you can never agree to do anything for them. They may be trapped in a book, talking loudly and angrily, but just let them be. That's what enchanted books do."

I put my hands on my hips and stare up at him. "Why

would I do anything for evil characters in a book? I'm not a baby, you know."

"I know." Ian exhales loudly. "It's just . . . well, many people, adults too, have been persuaded by these books to do bad things. And you aren't familiar with this world yet. You have a lot to learn and I wouldn't want you to make a mistake . . . I'm only trying to help."

I jut my chin out. "Maybe *we* don't want your help."

He glances away, and I see a bit of hurt in his expression. I consider apologizing as he pulls on a loose thread of his sweater, until he says, "I have to trust you with this . . . Can I trust you?"

My hands bunch into fists. When I answer him, I put venom in my words. "You can trust me. But can I trust *you?*"

"With what? Do you have something potentially life-altering in your room?" Ian shifts on his feet, scattering some loose papers in the small amount of space between us.

My back straightens and I huff. "With my dad. Whatever you did, wherever you went, you hurt him. Are you going to do it again?"

"*An enchanted child makes the old man quiet. Do you hear that, sister?*"

"*Shhh! I'm listening. It is time the old man faced punishment for his—*"

"I'm trying to make it up to him," he says, drowning out the voices.

"Whatever," I say.

I set the last book aside on the edge of the banister leading upstairs to our apartment. I can barely see the shop through the boxes and books. Sometimes there'll be a peek of empty shelves, black-and-white checkered floors in need of a serious mopping, or the fireplace that looks like it was carved in the 1600s for big cauldrons full of rabbit stew.

Just the thought of stew sets me further over the edge. I'm too hungry and way too annoyed to keep up with all of this. "I'm going out to get the pizza. I'll respect your stuff if you respect mine."

"Kaliope." Ian holds my gaze. "We're family. What's yours is mine."

"Family is open with one another. Until then, you're just Ian. Someone I don't know." I step back, bumping into the box.

"*I like her, sister.*"

"*Yes.*"

"Dad!" I call out. "Getting pizza. Be right back." I don't wait for his response as I grab his wallet on the counter and shimmy through the boxes and out onto the sidewalk. The glass door slowly shuts itself behind me, and I take a deep breath.

The lights on Main Street haven't gone out yet. I tuck my arms in a little closer against the chill. To my left, the bright green of the town square's grass pokes through the multicolored leaves that glow in the streetlamps. Above, there are gargoyles perched on every other rooftop. Totally weird. There's a wooden destination pole with arrows pointed to the Honeycrisp Hill elementary, middle, and high schools, the town hall, performing arts center, Honeycrisp Hill College, the Adachi estate, hospital, and library. They're all in the same direction, all within a half mile. Did they really need a sign for all that?

The shops to the right and across the street are all dark and deserted but one. I trudge over, stopping to look at fliers posted to poles and windows. There's an advertisement for the performing arts center's production of *Dracula at Christmas*, which sounds like *A Christmas Carol* meets Bram Stoker's classic and has everything: humor, family, and vampires! I chuckle, hand to my lips. Auditions on November 1. This town is so bizarre.

But . . . maybe I'll audition.

There's another ad for a Not-Thanksgiving Baking Competition & Festival:

For the fifth year, Honeycrisp Hill will host its Not-Thanksgiving Baking Competition & Festival in the town square! Instead of celebrating the colonization of America, you can spend time with your favorite townspeople eating delicious treats and bobbing for apples. All proceeds will go to the charities listed below. Sign up for the competition and booth allotment at Town Selectwoman Tina Avery's office! Can't wait to see you all there.

I take it back. The town's not bizarre, it's brilliant. I think I'm going to like it here.

My boots squelch, releasing a breath of cold air on my toes. Broken. Great. I bend down to check the new hole when my eyes catch on a display of cakes in a window. All kinds of baked masterpieces among autumn decorations, full of colors, both bright and muted, chocolate, vanilla, strawberry, lemon . . . They look so mouthwateringly good, it's enough for me to forget my shoe dilemma.

I look up. Wayward Sentiments Café & Sweetery. This is where Wini and her family work and live. I plaster my face to the window, trying to peek inside at any pastries left behind, but the cases in the back are empty. I can only make out jars of candy on the wall from the flickering light of a jack-o'-lantern left on, but can't read what their labels say. I can't wait to go inside there. If I can ever make my mouth say normal words to her, that is.

The chill nips at me once more and I remember what I came for. I shuffle past the bakery and the real estate office to the pizza place at the end of the block. A bell above the door jingles as I step inside, confronted by overwhelming heat and the thick scent of melting cheese. My stomach rumbles again.

They only sell pizza, which it says in big black letters above the counter. No salad. Soda. Breadsticks. Nada. *What does this look like? A restaurant?* But at least they have a million toppings. I step up to the vacated counter and ding a bell. Voices in the back drift out briefly before a tall, thin guy with an easy grin and vibrant red hair saunters up.

"Hiya there. I'm Russell. How many pizzas would you like?" His voice is a mixture of deep and whiny.

"Hi, Russell." I smile politely. "Can I get two pizzas? One with—"

Russell holds up a hand. "Nope, you don't gotta tell me what you want, kid. The oven knows your order."

"But how does it know?" I shake my head. This enchantment business doesn't make much sense. How would it know what I want when *I'm* not even sure what I want?

Russell shouts, "Two pies!" to no one in particular, and turns back to me, tilting his head to the side. "You're an enchanter. I can feel magic wafting off you. So can the oven. That's how it works. The oven senses you and knows what you want to eat. It's pretty simple and cuts down on food waste, let me tell you." He splays his hands against the counter and lowers his voice. "Your parents bought the bookstore, right?"

I don't have enough time to really understand what he said about the oven, but I have to keep up with the conversation. "Um, yeah. Well, my dad and grandpa?" I phrase it like a question even though it definitely isn't. My hands fidget and I move my feet on the linoleum too much.

Russell leans closer. "Right. I spoke to 'em. Maddie and Marcus were worried you'd be selling enchanted sweets, had to find out for them."

I frown. "Uh, no. Just books. Enchanted books."

"That's good." He frowns, though. "Business ain't so great at the bakery. Cost for extracted ingredients like Smart and Funny have gone up. Bad times for the Mosleys. Probably'll have to close."

I legit have no idea what any of that means so I just nod.

"So is it haunted?" he asks, eyes narrowed.

"The bookstore, you mean? No, no." I chuckle, stepping back. I hope these pizzas are done soon. I don't want to be here too much longer, answering weird questions. He merely *hmphs* and disappears through the kitchen doors. I'm grateful for the quiet.

I'm about to go look at some of the pamphlets scattered

on the far side of the counter when there's a rumbling outside like a storm.

I walk over to the window, noticing the streetlamps flickering. The heavy wind scatters leaves down the street and up against the window. The moon pokes through the clouds . . . and . . . and there's something there. Something above.

The tip of my nose presses into the glass and I stare at the shadow flying by the moon. I blink a few times, over and over. My mind and eyes must be playing a trick on me because what I'm seeing can't be real.

It's a . . . it looks like a cloaked . . . witch? It has a witch hat for sure, the kind that stores sell around Halloween. The shadow hovers beside the moon, darkening the sky over Honeycrisp Hill. And as I stare, I swear, for just a moment, that it's somehow looking at me. My skin prickles and bumps rise along my arms.

The witch sees me and moves closer, becoming smaller and smaller. More normal-size. More real. I gasp and back away from the window. It's coming for me. My heart pounds in my ears. My eyes widen and I'm about to scream when the doors burst open behind me. I twist around, mouth flapping open.

"Hey, you okay? You look like you've seen a ghost." Russell's got a big cheesy smile on his face. "Pizzas are ready."

"I . . ." is all I can manage to say. With a quick pivot, I look back out at the window but the witch is gone. The lights have stopped blinking. Everything's normal. The wind has died down and . . . I must have been imagining things.

"Do you need help getting back to the store, kiddo?"

I toss the money on the counter at Russell and take the pizzas from his hands. "N-n-no. I'm good."

"Hey, have a nice night! Stop by anytime. Be careful in that haunted shop," Russell calls after me. But his words barely register as I bolt outside, the pizzas sliding in the boxes. My cheeks burn as I sprint back to the bookshop.

My legs wobble, and my chest tightens to where breathing becomes difficult. And that's when the loop starts. *You're seeing things. You're silly. No one likes you. You're a joke.*

The world's a blur in my periphery. I imagine the gargoyles above follow my trajectory with interest. The shattering of glass somewhere only makes me swing the door shut behind me faster. I can't connect to anything else when the loop starts. For a solid ten minutes, all I can do is gasp for air.

I leave one of the pizzas—smoked salmon with dollops of cream cheese, chives, cherry tomatoes, pickled red onions, and . . . is that mango?—downstairs and run up to my room holding the other: a rainbow of usual (and unusual) veggies, which smells delicious even though the knots in my stomach twist.

"Girl . . . why do you cry? Do you not know the power inside of you?" The question is so soft, I almost believe I imagined it.

The loop pauses momentarily. I set the pizza down on the hallway bench and move closer to where the voice is coming from, tiptoeing toward it. "Who are you?"

"Violet," it says. It's coming from the bookshelf.

I stop at the edge of the shelf, my fingers grazing the wood on the very top, but I can't reach it. My breaths still come in pants, my heart racing. "Which book?"

"The Once Wicked." Her tone is gentle, innocent even.

"Never heard of it." My eyebrows scrunch together. "Are you one of Ian's enchanted books? I'm not supposed to talk to you."

"No, someone left me behind in the house, and very few have read my story," is the reply. *"I've been up here so long."*

The book must've indeed been left behind, because I don't remember Ian unpacking any of his personal collection yet. "That must be lonely."

"I do hear people outside sometimes . . ." She sighs. *"My apologies, I've been in such a foul mood up here on this shelf, without someone to talk to."*

I find myself nodding in understanding—that's how it's been for me for the past few years, too. Still, I have to ask the important questions. "Are you a wicked witch? Is that why your book is called *The Once Wicked*?"

There's a beat of silence. *"No, I'm not a witch. Though many who are stuck in books are witches."*

"Stuck?" My voice cracks a little, the terror that brought me up here slowly dissipating into curiosity. "But if you're stuck like wicked witches, doesn't that make you one?"

She laughs. *"Someone told me once that wicked is just another perspective."*

I step back, my boots scuffing the rug. "That seems like something only a wicked witch would say. Ian told me not to talk to the characters inside books. That they'll try to persuade me to do bad things."

"Perhaps some do . . . But I'm not a character. I'm an enchanter, like you. Besides, a wicked witch would ask you for something. Needle you into giving them whatever they want. I only want to listen to you, be your friend . . . if you'll let me."

I consider her words for a few moments. "Okay."

There's a smile in her tone when she speaks again. *"What's your name, friend?"*

"Kaliope," I answer. "You promise that you don't want me to set you free? You're not using me?"

"No." Her answer is quick. "I'm rather fond of my home, Kaliope. I only wish to be less alone. And maybe moved into a spot of sunlight. It's very dark without company."

I take a slice of pizza out and sit on the carpet below the book. "I know exactly what you mean."

7
Wini

There's something in the air, drifting through the crack in the window. Something new, wild. It smells like . . . change.

While change may not have a specific, memorable odor, it does contrast itself from everything else. Like being surrounded by the scent of cinnamon and brown sugar, and suddenly there's this faint whiff of oranges that grows more and more . . . It's different. Unexpected, yet welcome.

I'm not thinking sensibly *or* I'm just thinking about cinnamon orange pound cake.

I've been lying in bed, unable to sleep, thinking about my spell and where I might've gone wrong. Then I think about the shadow. And here's this smell of change, telling me I'm in trouble and I caused trouble. Or maybe I'm losing it. Probably too many hot chocolates. I wonder if four hot chocolates a day can rattle someone's mind enough to dream up shadowy figures haunting street corners?

With a groan, I swing my legs over the side of the bed and reluctantly cross the room to close the window. My footsteps fall softly on the old emerald rug I'd found at the town flea market a few years ago. It's a mixture between plush and scratchy. Old but timeless. My gaze catches on a cloud of voluminous curls outside. Aunt Maddie is taking out the garbage.

I watch her head back inside before turning toward my wobbly dresser. My fingers catch on the knob to my semi-broken Tiffany lamp and I twist, flooding a small radius in light good enough to read in. I should buy a new one, but the lamp's so pretty. My fashion has always been a bit more style over substance.

The clock tells me it's only 10:40 p.m.

Yeah, okay, a bit early for some on a Friday night, but I'm basically an eighty-year-old in a twelve-year-old's body. I plod over to the bookcase and grab the tome I've shoved behind all the others. The one I'm not supposed to have.

Grandma Bernice's journal, complete with untested spells. Its tattered leather cover stained a dark purple with our family name carved into it. The edges look like they've been singed, probably too close to a stove at one point, and the pages are thicker than parchment and infinitely older.

I flip it back open to *An Enchanted Match* and reread it for the millionth time.

Requirements: Level Nine magic.

Okay, I sort of fobbed that one. I can't be Level Nine until I'm thirteen and I pass the exam administered by the Enchantment Agency. I'm Level Eight anyway, have been for over a year, so I imagine that's close enough.

Three personal items (Stevie Wonder vinyl, Dad's list, and his favorite pastry), a drop of true love (the Jenkinses'), hair of an intended . . .

The directions are basic, and yeah, I tweaked it to imbue into the blueberry muffin bread, but I did the rest right, mostly. I mean, except for that whole hair thing, and maybe—definitely—my level of magic. And okay, she did say it didn't work, but it did. It brought the Enchantment Agency here.

I continue reading:

An Enchanted Match is a complex spell that should work in wondrous ways. The stronger the magic, the greater the effects. Casting this spell will create a series of events that will draw soulmates together and create recognition in each other. Beware; without a foundation, the magic will work in unpredictable ways.

Could possibly dissolve preexisting spells to finalize and stabilize itself.

What does *foundation* mean, anyway? I was hoping that without a person to source it into, it would grow into the *bread*. I slam the book shut and a flap of paper floats out of it, slowly drifting in the air before hitting the tips of my toes.

I set the book back on the shelf and snatch the paper.

Remember, Coraline,

Enchantment is the practice of good magic. Magic to make the world a better place and bring joy and meaning to all those who make and experience it. Enchantment cannot create that which does not exist, it can only build upon a foundation. And even then, it works in ways that you may never understand or intend. You must trust it.

Any magic that creates something where once there was nothing is dark. Forbidden. <u>Witchcraft</u>. You were born an enchanter. You were born a Mosley. Food may not be your medium, but no doubt there is something fated to be yours. Look toward the light, my darling. Never the dark.

Until then, learn to use this book. The spells within are challenging and require more magic than most of us possess. Like you, they are larger than life and require patience. Many don't work, at least they never did for me, but maybe with time, you can change them. You can complete them.

And remember, I love you, no matter where you go to find yourself.

Mama

I reread it over and over.

That smell of change hits my nostrils once again. Goose bumps rise along my arms. *Witchcraft*. Witches . . . they're real, I know that, but I've never seen one in my life. I just . . . I thought they were stories. Was Coraline looking into the dark? Was that why her spell . . . killed someone?

No one talks about wicked magic. I wouldn't even know how to perform it. Except . . . for . . . I think maybe I did?

The questions bounce around my brain like bubbles of boiling water.

And then something finally makes sense.

An Enchanted Match shouldn't have worked. I'm a good enchanter, but there was no foundation for this spell. I thought I could create one. Why *can't* I create love from nothing if I had good intentions? The absolute best intentions? Would that be wicked magic or would it be a new form of enchantment?

Suddenly, I realize the change that floated in wasn't about the world around me, but the world within me. Knowledge is a change in perspective, a change in what you knew before and what you know now. Knowledge is power.

I know what I want. I want to make the world a better place and bring meaning to people through food. That isn't dark. It can't be. I'm not a witch. I'm not Coraline.

I wrap my nightgown tight around my thighs as I pull the book back off the shelf and slide onto the edge of my bed. There's a desperation in me that needs to know more. To know where the lines lie between good magic—enchantment—and bad magic—witchcraft. Where I can and can't go. What are my limits? I don't want to steer toward the wickedness, I'm an enchanter through and through, and I believe Grandma Bernice. I will heed her warnings.

But I need to know everything if I can undo whatever I did before the Enchantment Agency finds out. They're already in town, soon they'll know it was me, and I'll be in serious trouble.

Out of the corner of my eye, I see the shadow outside my window, hovering in the patches of light between the trees of the woods. And there's that scent again.

Promising me that more is to come.

Recipe Journal of Winifred Mosley

BLACK PEPPER BISCUITS

Ingredients:

4 cups all-purpose flour

4 teaspoons baking powder

1 teaspoon baking soda

1 teaspoon salt

1 1/2 sticks butter

1 1/2 cups buttermilk

Whipping cream

Coarsely ground black pepper

Coarse sea salt for garnish (optional)

How to make:

1. Preheat oven to 450°F and line baking sheet with parchment paper.

2. Combine flour, baking powder, baking soda, and salt in a bowl and whisk together.

3. Add butter to the flour mixture and break apart with your fingers until the mix resembles coarse meal. Do not overwork!!! If it gets too warm, the butter will melt on your hands and that will not help your biscuits! Transfer to a large bowl.

4. Gradually add buttermilk until the dough comes

together in moist clumps. This is easiest if you use a fork and then softly mix with your hands.

5. Transfer to a lightly floured surface and pat into a 10-inch round pan, about 3/4 inches thick. Or until it looks right?

6. Using a biscuit cutter–or the rim of a medium-size glass–cut out 8-12 rounds.

7. Place the biscuits 2 inches apart on a parchment-lined baking sheet.

8. Brush the biscuits with whipping cream and sprinkle with ground pepper and maybe some sea salt, but not the large granules.

9. Bake the biscuits for 15-18 minutes.

10. Brush with a little melted butter if you like OR wait for them to cool and slice them open for a delicious sandwich. My personal favorites: prosciutto with Manchego cheese and a little fig jam if you've got it, or if you're not a meat eater, pan grill the biscuits with mozzarella and red pepper aioli, maybe some red chili flakes? Or keep it simple, just cheese or whatever. I personally don't think tuna tastes that great on biscuits, but that's just me. Is this too much info for a recipe? Annnnnyway, enjoy your biscuits!

8

Kal

My favorite Della song streams out of my radio, and I roll over, hitting the off button. I throw off my weighted blanket and notice I'm still in my regular clothes. I must've forgotten to change into my pajamas after being too stuffed from pizza. Guess Dad never came to check in on me, either. What a surprise.

I grunt, stretching my arms above my head and yawning at the same time.

"Kaliope?" Violet whispers. I sit up quickly and stare at the book that's now sitting on the windowsill, basking in the morning light. I don't remember taking it into my room, but then, I was really upset yesterday and it was nice to have a friend. It was nice to have someone who listens.

"Hi, Violet." I gingerly swoop my legs over the side of the bed and stand up. "How's the morning light? Better than the top of a dusty bookcase?" I stifle another yawn.

"Much better," she says cheerfully. *"I can't see much, but I can feel warmth."*

I rub the tiredness from my eyes. "You can see and feel?"

She pauses a moment while I get myself in gear. *"I*

can see a little of what's around me. I can feel the sunlight warming my covers."

That makes sense. "That's cool." I dart through a few boxes of my old photos, my own collection of books I bought from various library sales, and funky band posters. There are three suitcases full of my clothes in front of the dresser. With another stretch, I bend down and pull out a pair of ripped jeans and a black T-shirt. My wardrobe, except for my accessories, is sort of basic, but finding time and money to go shopping has been difficult. Thankfully, I haven't grown too much in the past year, otherwise I'd have nothing. As I slide into the jeans, a thought occurs to me. "You said you were an enchanter, right?"

Violet's voice perks up. *"That's correct. I was."*

"What kind were you?" I lower the shirt over my head and grimace at my bushy hair sticking up all over the place in the mirror.

"Words, like your family. My family was very good at writing new spells. That's why we owned this very bookshop."

I pause for a second. "Your family owned the bookstore? And they left you behind?"

"No," Violet says quickly. *"Well, yes. I had many siblings and one of their children being stuck in a book . . . it's easy to forget. They never did come back, though. I suspect they didn't really want me."*

I nod, brushing out the last of my tangled hair. "I know what you mean."

I've been forgotten many times by Dad and by friends at school. When you're different and tend to panic in new situations, people sometimes forget you exist. Or worse, they pretend you don't. "Hey, I gotta go to enchanter school. If my—if Ian or my dad come through, be really quiet, okay? I don't think they'd like me talking to a book. I don't think they'd understand."

"Of course, Kaliope. I'll be very quiet." In a softer voice, she adds, *"I can help you with enchanting, if you like. We don't have to tell anyone."*

Something about the way she says that makes my stomach sink a bit, or maybe I'm hungry. Maybe I'm just reading into things. "I . . . I'd like that."

"I'm happy to hear it," she says with a hint of genuine joy. *"And good luck at school today. Remember, everyone starts somewhere, and you're more powerful than you even know."*

"Thanks, Violet. I'll try to remember that." I take a deep breath before grabbing my backpack and bounding out of my room. The door whooshes shut behind me. I head toward the kitchen to grab a snack or cereal or something but the place is a mess. And the pizza is all gone, too.

I grumble and head downstairs into the bookstore. At

the bottom, my feet freeze on the stairs. The shelves are nearly full and organized. There's a pile of empty boxes stacked in the back half of the shop, and Dad's sitting on the floor, surrounded by books.

When he senses my presence, he turns around and smiles. He's got shadows under his eyes, his hair is disheveled, and his glasses hang askew. He's in the same clothes as yesterday. Suddenly, him not checking on me last night makes sense. He did this—all of this—by himself.

"Where's Ian?" I try not to sound angry, but it slips into my question anyway.

Dad sighs, the smile still hanging on his lips. "Think he just got back from picking up a few more grimoires from the distributor in Boston. He's around somewhere." He looks me up and down. "How'd you sleep? How are you feeling?"

"Fine," I say, taking another step down. "Better than you, I guess."

He shrugs. "Wanted to get this place ready so we can focus on the good things like hanging out and meeting people. Spending time together, just you and me." There's a sparkle of hope in his tone, and I want to match it, but I'm wary.

I cock an eyebrow. "Are you sure you have time for that?"

"Once all of this is settled, I'll have plenty of time, kiddo. You're probably gonna get sick of me." He sets a huge tome of spells on the floor. "I forgot to mention, I made an appointment with a new psychologist in town for Tuesday after school. She sounds pretty cool and got your files from Jenny."

I exhale slowly. I knew that moving would mean having new doctors, but I'm going to miss Jenny. And starting over again means I'll have to tell the new doctor all the weird stuff and hope she doesn't judge me.

When Dad notices me nibbling my lip, he hurries over and wraps me in a hug.

"I know it's a lot, and I know I've said that many times now, but you aren't alone." He lifts me off my feet and holds me close. I shut my eyes, enjoying the warmth. "You'll see, you'll be happy here. It's going to be different."

We stay like that for a few moments, and I feel good. I feel better. Maybe it is going to be okay; maybe I will be happy here. He sets me back on my feet.

"Good luck at enchanter school today. And hey, you'll see Wini there. At least you'll know someone." He goes back to his books and I walk toward the door. "Bye, honey."

I open the door and the bells chime as the cool air hits my cheeks.

Right. Enchanting. I can totally do this . . . and maybe Wini won't hate me like she did yesterday. Or better yet, maybe I'll make different friends, ones whose dads don't seem interested in mine.

I shake my head. That's a good plan. Now all I have to do is get there and not get lost trying to find this weird school on a weird street in this weird town. Out of the corner of my eye, I glimpse Ian on the sidewalk with a bunch of boxes, and I really don't want to deal with him right now so I ignore him and step in the opposite direction. Thankfully, I look away just in time to see Wini darting down the street. Great, I'll just follow her.

Here goes nothing.

9

Wini

The clock reads seven a.m. I resist the urge to rub the sleep from my eyes as I finish writing up a recipe in the journal, cast my spell, and shove biscuits into my waiting lunch box. Saturday school isn't the worst, except it's too early.

I'd rather be here, doing what I do best. Where I feel best. This bakery is all I know. The only place I belong. What if the Enchantment Agency takes me away from it because I did magic I wasn't supposed to?

My fingers drift down my velvet black dress with a white circle neckline. With my bright red glasses and curls tumbling down my shoulders, I think I make it look very chic. I zip up my boots, cinch my trench coat, and strap my purple shoulder bag across my body. I take a deep breath. Every time I leave this bakeshop, I feel like I'm putting on armor.

Sometimes it feels like the world is very much against me because of Coraline, even though I'm nothing like her. I would never hurt someone on purpose or be wicked. I would never abandon my family.

I head out the door and down the street as the shops prepare for opening. Some neighbors scuttle by, their words drifting past me.

"The air feels different . . . colder, right?"

"The weather's stormier, too, and I swear . . ."

I cringe, trying to listen to more, but they're too far away now. Are these things happening because I called a wickedness to town? This can't be good. Out of the corner of my eye, I see the Enchantment Agency lady on the opposite side of the street, holding out a long metal stick—a wand?—and waving it around. I can only guess what it does, but no doubt she's trying to trace errant magic.

I pick up my pace and look away, not wanting her to pay attention to me. I peek over at the bookshop. The older man with fluffy white hair and piercing green eyes sorts through the million boxes all over the sidewalk. Inside, there's not a ghost in sight, though I do see Kal and her dad hugging.

Ian waves at me, and I awkwardly wave back and speed off down the street before he tries to talk to me or something. I bet their shop will do well, at least better than our bakery.

Aunt Maddie used to say it's a rough patch. That it happens, and we just need to step up our game, do something new. We did that and it didn't help. Now

Maddie says nothing. Dad says people no longer want our product and it's time to stop offering it before we're bankrupt.

All I know is that if we lose the bakery, we lose Grandma Bernice's dream, and we lose our home. So I have to believe we still have a chance. There are too many new trends in baking that we haven't explored. When it's my turn to run the shop, I'm going to keep it fresh *and* classic. Make my own recipes and tweak the older ones.

Of course, that's only if I fix An Enchanted Match.

I set those thoughts aside as I pass by the high school and down the crooked dead-end lane with houses hidden by trees that stretch high into the sky. Leaves skitter in my path, and there's a whisper.

Winifred . . .

I twist around. Am I hearing things?

The wind whips up and the trees begin to sway. My pace quickens as darkness falls around me; black-gray clouds flood the sky. The sidewalks crack unevenly beneath my feet.

Winifred . . .

Now I'm running, my strides unsure, my breath coming in short bursts. Something's following me, and whatever it is . . . it's wicked.

And it's after me.

Shuttered windows flap open in the wild wind, the

whispers grow to a crescendo in my ears, and my feet catch on the edge of the curb, just outside the bright blue Victorian at the end of the block. I wave my arms to find balance. As I do, the darkness retreats and the sun pokes through the dissipating clouds. The sky's a brilliant blue, the wind is quiet, and the sidewalk is straight and flat like always.

With my body bent over at the waist, I inhale greedily. And then there's a hand on my shoulder and I flail around with a screech, only to see it's Kal. She's wearing the same clothes as the other day, and I see a peek of her bright blue socks through a broken flap in her boots.

She huffs, as if she was running behind me. "Whoa, are you okay?"

Get yourself together, I tell myself, straightening. Everything's so normal now, I can't even grasp that anything just happened. But . . . I do know what happened. I messed up the spell and now something scary and bad is coming, and it's getting worse.

"I'm fine, sorry. Just got a bit spooked by . . . uh . . . something." I shake my head. Of all the things I could've said. No way she's going to be my friend now. Plus, she doesn't really respect food enchantment, though maybe I'm reading that wrong.

"Oh . . . okay," Kal says, looking up at the Victorian with its wrap-around porch crowded by seven cats of various colors. My favorite one, Midas, who's a shocking gold and wears a little plaid bow tie, rises on his hind legs and saunters over to the steps, awaiting my ascent.

I bend down at the top of the stairs to pet his silky fur while he purrs his approval and I continue to catch my breath. He rubs the side of his face against my knees a few times and then heads off mysteriously to wherever he goes while I'm stuck in class. Probably to laze in the last patches of autumn sunlight.

"What's with all these cats?" Kal steps up the stairs, and one by one all the cats look at her.

"The cats are part of the Honeycrisp Hill *meowfia*. They congregate wherever there's treats and magic. They really like shiny things, too, so keep your valuables close." I wave her up, wondering if she saw me running down the street like a weirdo. If she did, she's not saying. "So you have Saturday Enchantment, too?"

"Uh, yeah. But like . . . I mean, I'm not good. I don't know anything. When I said I tried a spell and got the food part right, it was a total fluke. Not that you asked or anything." She barely takes a breath between this stream of words as she joins me on the porch. She's almost my height, which is saying something, as I'm always the tallest in the room.

"Don't worry about it. That's why we go to class, right?"

"But . . . is that the point of Saturday school? I'm try-ing to understand why we have to go."

"The Enchantment Agency made school mandatory if we want to practice enchantment on our own and get our license. They also use it to make sure we don't cause any major catastrophes. You'll read about it in the Enchantment Agency lawbook we all get." I don't know why, but I find myself smiling. It's been a long time since someone in this town looked at me without knowing my history.

Her eyes widen. "What happens if we cause major catastrophes?"

"They send you to magical jail or strip you of your magic if you're *really* bad—so I've heard. I mean, it's rare anyone causes major catastrophes, so there's not much to worry about." I wink at her, waiting till she seems less fretful and her shoulders unhunch before turning away. I really hope I didn't cause a major catastrophe.

I swallow the sudden lump in my throat that comes from the thought of getting my magic stripped away and press the doorbell. The chimes are to the tune of *The Worst Witch* score.

Kal's eyebrows raise.

"Ms. Baird's a huge fan. Don't ask about it unless you want to be here for hours after class."

Kal giggles as the door opens on its own. "How . . . ?"

I don't know where to start. Enchantment is magic, and magic is everywhere, in each little crevice and pocket of the world. Maybe even the universe . . . but that's too much to tell a newbie right away. All I say is, "It's the way our world works. You'll see."

Kal slowly steps in behind me just as the door swings shut. She stops, head tilted back. The wooden floor beneath her feet squeaks as her eyes widen to take in all the sights. Sometimes I forget how strange this place must look to someone who hasn't been here a million times.

There's a grand wooden staircase in the center that travels up to a darkened hallway—students aren't allowed up there. On the wall are portraits of various enchanters from history. My personal favorite is Wanda Morrow, who is as Black and chunky as me and wears a bright purple spandex jumpsuit. The air around her sparkles like a rainbow.

Wanda's my hero. Not only could she enchant the sky to rain when there was a drought or cool during a long heatwave, but she could even make the stars wink to the beats of her favorite songs. I've spent hours staring at her portrait, hoping one day my own portrait would be hanging next to it.

None of this is what captures Kal's attention, though. It's the circular table hanging from the ceiling holding a vase of lilacs that's got her mouth dropping open. I'll admit, the whole defying-gravity thing is surprising to some, but what gets me is that the flowers haven't died. In fact, they smell just as nice since the table turned upside down. If only I could figure out how to do that with doughnuts.

"How . . . ?" The word escapes her lips like a surprise.

"Spells go wrong." What I don't mention is that my mom was the one to do it. That even then, at my age, she was ridiculously powerful. And making mistakes . . . like me. I shrug and nod in the direction of the open classroom door to our right. "We've got two minutes. Ms. Baird will enchant our clothes into sailor costumes if you're late, and blue and white stripes don't look good on me."

Kal turns to me, a big grin transforming her face. "This place is bizarre."

"You have no idea," I toss over my shoulder as we head into the classroom. Kal's a fair distance behind me, and while I'd like to help her navigate the room, it's better if she makes up her own mind where she wants to go. And who she wants to hang with.

The classroom is only half full, decorated with posters of enchanters doing spells safely and confidently. Most of the students sit in the back in old-school wooden desks that you can open and stick books inside. The matching chairs are freestanding, but also dangerous. Sometimes they'll shimmy out from beneath you to dance or sometimes you'll sink through them as they've suddenly decided to change their density.

Number one rule of Saturday school: Tap your seat before plopping your butt down. It can save you a little injury and a ton of embarrassment.

That's exactly what I do as I take the desk in the second row—as far away from everyone else as I can.

Kal stands at the front of the classroom, eyeing the open spaces. Her leather jacket and torn jeans stand out, but in the coolest way possible. She smiles my way and I return it. She approaches the chair near mine, and I'm about to tell her to tap it first when a voice cuts me off.

"Hey, new girl, come sit with us," Janet Hearst calls out from the back of the room, where she's clustered among her gaggle of friends. "You don't want to hang with Betty Crocker, believe me."

Kal's eyes dart to mine and I give her a nod, telling her it's okay. She wants to sit with the cool kids, I get it. Even if she doesn't know me, she can tell I won't make her popular at school.

A sigh escapes softly as she takes a seat in the back. And then there's chatter as they all introduce themselves at once. I don't hear Kal's replies but I'm happy when Ms. Baird comes in, her red hair in a perfect bee-hive. Her outfit's the usual—a black shift dress with red heels and dangly earrings.

"Hello, everyone." She elongates the O and takes a sip of tea from a floral mug on her desk. "First things first, the Enchantment Agency is in town and is requesting all enchantment students report any recent experiences that seem odd or if you've seen anything that seems, well, spooky, to their agent . . . a Miss Diaz, in the temporary office across from the town square. So there you have it. Also!" Her eyes light up and her beehive seems to grow a few inches. Meanwhile, I feel a bit sick to my stomach at the mention of the Agency. "We have a new student. Kaliope Clarke, care to introduce yourself and your medium?"

A chair in the back scrapes against the floor, and Kal rises. I notice her hands fidget a bit.

"Hi, I'm Kaliope Clarke. You can call me Kal. Um . . . I'm from Boston. Well, I mean, that's where I was born. My medium is words, I think? My dad's medium is words, same with my grandma and grandpa. I never had a chance to practice and find out what I'm best at . . . so this is all really new to me. And I'm so excited because I feel like I'm going to do well at it and just, like . . . be awesome, you know?" There's a dreaminess in her voice. She smiles before falling straight through her chair and onto the floor. Her jeans rip a bit more over her left knee. Her face is bright red.

Janet's friends laugh hysterically while I fight the urge to bolt to my feet and give her my hand. Ms. Baird crosses the room and pulls Kal up, glaring at the other students.

"The chairs here aren't to be trusted. Are you all right, dear?" Ms. Baird asks as Kal dusts her pants off.

"I'm fine." Her voice wobbles.

"It has happened," Ms. Baird states with an edge to her tone meant to silence the laughter, "to everyone in this room at least twice. Now, come sit up here. You'll find the company is far more mature."

Ms. Baird sets Kal's bag on the desk beside mine and winks at me briefly before Kal stalks back this way. I turn away, not sure if I should try again at this whole friendship thing. I know better than to get my hopes up. Besides, maybe she wants to be cool. Maybe she's seen enough of me to know we don't fit.

"Now, I want you all to turn to the person next to you," Ms. Baird says, stepping up to the chalkboard. "For the next two weeks, you will work together on a Halloween class project."

My hand pops up.

Ms. Baird huffs, not turning around. How does she always know? "Yes, Ms. Mosley?"

"Is it possible to do this assignment by myself?"

Her response comes quickly. "No."

I grimace while my eyes slide over to Kal. She seems nice and I want to like her, but if I'm going to undo An Enchanted Match, I can't work with a total newbie to magic. I can't work with anyone. I'm about to say that the bakeshop needs me, which'll make group work hard, when Ms. Baird seems to read my mind.

"Winifred Mosley. You will work with Kaliope Clarke, understood? And I swear, if you write me another strongly worded email in the 'best interest of pedagogical enlightenment,' I will give you a zero."

My jaw drops in indignation. "That's not fair! I have—"

"Not. Another. Word." Ms. Baird clears her voice before continuing. "Now, the project. It'll be about the most best-intentioned spell you can create to positively impact a person's life. I don't want you to perform the spell, but I want you to compose it with your partner. Okay?" There's a collective groan around the room, my own adding to the cacophony.

The only person not joining in is the new girl, whose cheeks are still rosy.

And then it's like a light bulb goes off and the perfect project idea pops up, one that'll feed two birds with one scone.

An Enchanted Match.

It'll definitely—and positively—impact a person's life if I fix it and get rid of the wickedness I accidentally called to town. *And* if it works, there's no way our bakery can fail. There's no way it won't bring in new customers seeking new emotions, especially love.

Love. The thought swirls inside my mind like a cinnamon roll. If I'm creating it for good, life-altering reasons, it can't be wicked magic, right? It can't be witchcraft, and even if it is, it can't be bad or . . . wicked.

My hand thrusts into the air once more.

"Yes, Ms. Mosley?" Ms. Baird's voice is annoyed, but I'm about to surprise both of us, so she needs to calm down.

"Does this mean we'll have access to library books?" I try to keep the excitement from my voice. The library has all sorts of ancient grimoires with old spells—surely one of those could help me make sense of the spell I cast and how it went wrong.

Ms. Baird turns around to stare at me as if she can figure out my motivations with a glance. Ha, good luck at that. "No. There are too many books up there that aren't for your age group." Her lips twist and I deflate a little into my seat. "But . . . I imagine between the Clarke family grimoires and their new bookstore, you'll have plenty of new material to peruse, right?"

I lean back in my chair.

I sneak a glance at Kal. Her lips scrunch together as she stares down at a notebook, her pen dangling over its empty lines. She's pouting, with a far-off look in her eyes. I bet she's daydreaming. I've seen that look on Aunt Maddie sometimes while she's standing in the middle of the kitchen, a million things baking around her. Dreamers are my favorite kind of people. To believe in impossible things and try to make those things happen . . .

My fingers thrum against my desk. Fine. Challenge accepted. I can work with Kal on some unimportant spell, and in the process, I'll get my hands on books that I haven't seen before in her store. I'll figure out An Enchanted Match on my own.

I'll save the bakery and the town from whatever wickedness I called before the Enchantment Agency finds out it was me and takes away my magic and locks me up in a magical prison.

Easy peasy.

10

Kal

My stomach grumbles. I didn't know I needed to bring lunch—not that we have anything in the fridge back home. Can't believe neither Dad nor Ian went shopping, ugh.

"I have extra if you want?" Wini tosses me a glance, half annoyed, I think. Her fingers tap on her Star Wars lunch box.

I shake my head, feeling guilty and embarrassed about earlier. She was really kind to me, but then I sort of abandoned her. Then she was a bit weird about working with me . . . which means she probably can't stand my guts now. "No, it's cool. I'm—"

"You a vegetarian?"

"Uh, no."

"Lactose intolerant?"

"No." I shift in my seat, glad not to fall through another one again.

"Gluten-free?"

"Nope."

"On a . . . a diet?" She shudders as if it's a dirty word.

I shake my head, trying not to laugh.

"Take it." She slides a biscuit with something that looks like ham, cheese, and a fancy jam in between. She doesn't say another word. And wow, if that biscuit sandwich isn't the real deal. I even lick my fingers after. I could probably eat one of those every day for the rest of my life.

Before I can thank her, Ms. Baird waves me over while assigning everyone else reading from the textbook. For the next few hours, she explains basic things I should have known since I was five, as she tells me nothing short of six times. She also has me sign some paperwork and hands me a card that says I'm allowed to practice low-level magic without supervision. Anything above that requires an adult. It makes me feel like a baby, but as Violet said, you have to start somewhere. And maybe I will be more powerful than I think.

She points out a few spells in the textbook. "See right there, where it says 'LVL' and the number? You can do any of those that are three and under. When enchanters do spells above their level, they run the risk of exhausting their magic. It could be days, weeks, even years before you'd get it back, okay?"

I nod my head. "Wow, I didn't know that."

"Of course you didn't," she says with a smile. "That's why you're learning now."

By the time school is over, I've got a crap ton of home-work and a project. Double ugh.

As we're packing up, Wini takes a step toward me. "We should talk. Come on."

We stride beneath the table hanging upside down as the other students filter past us, eager to get back home.

"Right. So . . . today was weird," she says as we step onto the porch, and the cats begin circling our legs.

The sun's peeking through the cloudy sky as if to offer a bit of hope. And I need hope, a lot of it. I'm constantly swinging between being excited for a new life and the realization that I still am not good enough, right enough. It's giving me whiplash.

"I know I'm not your first choice as a partner, but I promise I'm a fast learner and I—" I begin until she cuts me off.

"I don't like working with anyone—this town's not a fan of me. But if I had to work with someone, I'm happy to work with you." A long breath lands between us as if she's nervous about the conversation.

My brow furrows as I try to figure out what to say. I'm glad I get to work with her, too, especially after Janet and the others laughed at me. But I can't say that. "So what should we do?" I adjust the straps of my backpack while we mosey down the street into the town square. In the center, there's a lifelike statue of a man wearing a fall jacket. The soggy bright green grass slicks the tops of my boots.

"I have all of my grandma's old lesson plans from when she taught my dad and aunt, so I can teach you at the same time as we work on our project. You can figure out what you want to do and I'll help you get good enough to write a spell. But I have a few questions."

"Ask away." I stop in my tracks beside the strange statue, the man's face contorted in horror. Someone must've put a plaid fall jacket on him, which is just . . . odd. I trace my fingers along the statue's shoulder.

"Hey! Don't touch him!" an old man sweeping leaves across the street yells. "Derrick is very sensitive."

"Sorry!" I yank my hand off and back away. The statue's named Derrick and he's sensitive. *Okay* . . .

Wini ignores the entire scene as she roots around her backpack. "First, you eat this." She holds out a little translucent bag with a chocolate truffle inside.

I eye her warily but take it. "Is this . . . enchanted?"

"Yep." She holds my gaze. "We can't spare the enchantment ingredients, they're ridiculously expensive. But I want you to see what enchanted food can do. This is a Patient Praline. It's got melty caramel inside, a bit of sea salt on top, and Patience extract."

I purse my lips, feeling suddenly nervous. My raggedy boots shift on the stone. "If I eat this, I'll feel patient?"

She tosses her head side to side. "You'll feel calm, only for a few hours as opposed to a full day. It's not quite as long-lasting or strong on enchanters as it is on humans."

"But I'll be in control, though, right?" I know I ask that in a weird way, and she probably thinks I have control issues or something, which I absolutely do. My anxiety makes me feel like if I'm not exactly sad or bubbly, I'll spiral into something totally else.

Her sparkly boots contrast so wildly with the rest of the town and the grayness flooding the sky. "Yes, but honestly, it can't hurt you to feel calm as you begin lessons with me. It's a lot to take in and overwhelming, you know? Magic demands patience."

I nod and pop the chocolate in my mouth, hopefully swallowing down all my fear with it. My eyes close and I suddenly feel good, like everything's going to be okay. My limbs feel looser and my heart beats nice and steady. "Wow."

"It works fast, right?" Her voice carries a smile. "I made those myself from my own recipe. It could be a new bestseller in our shop . . . if people actually came in. How do you feel?"

"Unlike myself, but in a good way? Relieved?" I open my eyes and let out a long, lovely breath.

"Good," she says with a nod. "Now repeat after me,

'Heart and mind, body and soul, shimmer bright what hides in sight.'"

My nose crinkles as I say each word slowly. Wini waits till I'm done and steps closer. "Only the caster can glimpse how the words enchant, so what do you see?"

At first I see nothing, and then there's an explosion of color around me, circling my hands and body like mist. I try to keep the awe from my voice. "Colors. Blue—"

She gestures to keep going. "That means calm, hopeful. What else?"

"Yellow, maybe?" I squint. "They're all mashed together."

"That's normal for your first time. Now I want you to look harder, focus. Try to pick the colors apart. Read them like . . ." She smiles. "Like a book."

That earns her a snort. "Okay, okay. There's green and red, orange, yellow, blue . . . It's like a spectrum all around me, all mixed up. Way too many to see." I shake my head, suddenly overwhelmed. "I'm sorry."

Her smile is replaced by a grimace. "Hmm." Her head tilts back and she's staring up at the sky like she can find the right words there. Thunder cracks overhead, startling me, and Wini's eyes widen. The air turns colder, and I hug my arms closer. A myriad of emotions floods her face.

I step closer to her, shutting out the townsfolk milling around us. "Do you want to tell me what you're thinking or what?" My lips tighten into a frown. "Are you disappointed in my magic?"

"No," Wini says, still looking upward, brow furrowed. "Sorry, I was just thinking about . . . something else." She tears her gaze away from the sky and looks at me.

I shift in my broken boots, waiting for her to talk.

"You ever feel like . . . you don't belong somewhere, but at the same time, you really want to, but you keep messing it up?" Her voice comes out soft and almost sad.

"Yeah," I admit. Wasn't I there just last week? I always wanted to belong somewhere, but I could never tell anyone I was an enchanter. I couldn't even talk much about what I went through with my mental illness. I'm always holding back. I came here to belong. To be whole.

"I might've made a big mistake," Wini says suddenly as the first raindrop plops on the ground. Then she stands straighter and plasters a smile on her face. "Anyway, we should—"

I extend my hand out to her. "Be friends?"

"Really? You're going to find out that people in town don't like me and—"

That's the second time she mentioned this and hasn't said why. I'm not sure she wants me to ask either, so I reach out and take her hand in mine. She grips it gently like she could break me, and I stifle a laugh. "We're friends now. Who cares about what everyone else thinks? I know I took a seat in the back today, but in my defense, you seemed like you wanted me to. So now we're friends and I can . . . help you with your big mistake, if you want." I try not to sound too desperate.

"Oh no, that's for me to fix." She swings her other hand around as if she's batting whatever mistake she made away. When she smiles again, this time it lights up her entire face even as the sky turns darker and stormier. "Friends. I'd like that." She lets my hand drop. "Well, friend, how about we meet later at your bookstore? We can grab a few of your family grimoires and start learning magic."

"Sure," I say. "That sounds great." Though I'm a bit disappointed she doesn't want me to help her with her mistake. I probably have to earn her trust first. Get to know her. Then she'll let me in.

She gives me a two-finger wave and darts off. And I stand there, lost in thought as the raindrops get plumper and soak through my hat. This place . . . it's small and it's totally weird—from Derrick the statue and Saturday school, to Wini Mosley, to our "haunted" bookstore and my new grandfather who comes with emotional baggage and talking books.

But maybe, just maybe, Honeycrisp Hill's not going to be so bad after all.

It just needs a little love and something new.

I can't wait to go home and tell Violet.

The old man who yelled at me rushes across the street, pushing me aside. "Derrick's terrified of lightning and hates the rain." He starts to lower a tarp over the statue. I stumble out of his way, but I'm unbothered.

Things are changing for me in this weird, perfect little town. I'm no longer alone. I'm no longer powerless. I have a friend. A real-person friend.

It's going to be okay. *I'm* going to be okay.

11

Wini

"Dad? Hello?" I dump my backpack by the stairs and turn around in the bakeshop twice. How is he not here? Saturdays are his favorite. It's quiet, with more time for low-key interaction with out-of-town customers.

"Dad!"

I start up the stairs when Maddie calls out.

"He's out for the day. Come here."

The air's sweet and floral in the front of the house, but heavy with delicious pastries warming on racks. The bakeshop's in full swing for no reason at all other than tradition.

"Where is he?" I tie my apron and then squat to stare at my reflection in the glass display case. My adorable polka-dot bandanna covers my curls enough to keep them out of the food.

"He had some business on the other side of town," Maddie says, wiping down a table with a towel.

"Dad doesn't have business."

Maddie shoots me the side-eye. "Little girl," she says,

which is code for *child who is trying to act grown*, "your father has a life outside of you, you know?"

"I know." I cringe. "I didn't mean it like that. I just wanted to talk to him is all."

"Why, what do you need?" She touches her fingers to the dead tea light that sits inside one of the jack-o'-lanterns. Must have been on all night. *"With my magic I do implore, enchant this light, its energy restore,"* she whispers, and the light flickers on. "What, you got an A-minus? Oh no . . ." Her tone is mocking.

I roll my eyes and throw my hands up with a huff. "Why are you always so mean?"

Maddie smirks. "Oh, you're sensitive today."

I shake my head. I don't usually do this, but that's the last straw. All the stress and pressure of the spell going wrong and losing the bakery . . . it's too much. "You're hurting my feelings, Auntie."

Maddie puts the pumpkin back and stands tall. Her face wilts, the humor gone. "You're right, that was mean. I'm sorry, and I didn't mean to hurt your feelings. What happened?"

When I was younger, she used to make her jokes and tell me to suck it up, but after a while, I told her that wasn't okay. Since then, she tries to meet me halfway and listen.

"The new girl who moved into the bookstore down the way—"

"The haunted one?" Maddie interrupts, eyes round.

"I don't think it's haunted. Anyway, what I was saying is I have to do a school project with her and she agreed to be my friend but I don't want to blow it, so I needed Dad's advice."

My aunt looks at me for a solid minute before she finally smiles. "That's great, Wini. Is she coming over today? Do you want me to make you snacks? Everyone likes each other a lot better when they're well-fed."

Before I can answer, the door to the bakery jingles open and in steps Dad—and Lachlan.

Dad's lips purse to keep a smile at bay. "How good are you at kneading bread?"

Kal's dad chuckles softly. He's relaxed and his body is angled toward my dad, his dimples working overtime. "I'm substantially better when the company's good."

Oh my God. They're flirting. I want to jump for joy and shove them together. *Yessss*, Dad! I've never seen him so happy and carefree. I stand there, frozen next to Maddie, both of us afraid if we move or say anything, Dad will reconsider the whole thing.

"Well, I'd better go see Kal and help my old man with the store." Lachlan leans against the doorway.

Dad nervously wraps his arms over his chest. "If you need any help, let me know. I'm great at organizing."

"You know what, I might take you up on that." Lachlan gives him a big, goofy smile and then takes off into the rain. Dad stares after him, his own smile tugging at his cheeks.

When he finally turns around, his face drops and turns the only rosy shade possible with such dark skin.

Aunt Maddie's the first to talk. "Good for you."

I grin. "Very cool, Dad. He seems nice." Though part of me does worry that if Dad and Lachlan date or whatever, there's a chance things might go poorly and then me and Kal can't be friends . . . We'll cross that bridge when we get to it. "Dad, I need your help."

He nods, his lips twisting. "What is it, my love?"

When I tell him everything (except my impending doom with the Enchantment Agency because of An Enchanted Match, which may be the reason he and Lachlan are getting along so well, which would be really, really bad), he scrubs his chin.

"Go over to the bookstore and be your lovely normal self." Dad pats my shoulder. "She wants to be your friend, Wini. You got this. But definitely take some snacks."

"See, snacks always work." Aunt Maddie beams with pride. I'm about to find out what's in the kitchen when her lips curve into a pout. "Did you all hear about the Enchantment Agency in town? Their agent has been interviewing everyone, and for some reason, she's been asking questions about us, too."

Dad *hmmms*. "Well, that's weird."

My entire body cringes. She's getting closer to figuring out it was me. I have to do something fast. I have to stop An Enchanted Match before it's traced back to me. "Oh, yeah, wonder why . . ." Even to my own ears, I sound shady and secretive.

But neither Maddie nor Dad seem to notice.

"It is weird," Auntie agrees. "Just as weird as what's been going on around town. People have been talking about shadows and patches of frigid air. They think something is seriously wrong, and that . . . well . . ." She glances between the two of us. "This is exactly how it was just before Coraline cast her curse."

Nerves flutter in my stomach. What could that mean?

An hour later, I wait in the bookstore for Kal to come downstairs.

My legs sneakily carry me over to the back of the store that has a metal card hanging from the ceiling stating HIGHER LEVEL MAGIC. The shelves are packed with what look like rare grimoires with tatty, crinkly covers and almost illegible titles. Carefully, I touch the spine of one, the sparks of magic tingling the tips of my fingers. Within my grasp, there's power and spells I've never seen before. Spells that could change my world. Make me better than others. Make me better than my mother. Fix everything.

I tuck my hands back into my pockets.

You don't touch unknown magical books without permission. Besides, I'd get in trouble just looking at higher-level magic spells. No, I will do it the right, respectful way.

I'm not my mother. Even if I may have done something wicked.

I settle myself on a box when voices begin whispering through the walls and stacks of boxes.

"Do you feel that, sister?" The tone is singsongy, sending chills down my spine.

"Yes," someone—something—hisses in response. *"Power."*

My hands grip my knees and my eyes widen. I swallow the scream creeping up my throat. It's not real. It can't be.

"We must—"

"Don't mind the voices, dear," Ian says, startling me out of my skin. I jump, my shoulder bag thudding onto the floor. A gargled whimper is the only response I can make. "There, there." He picks up my bag and raises his hands in the international gesture of *calm down*.

"It's really haunted?"

Ian laughs, taking a step back and scooping a stack

of magazines from within an open box. "No, of course not. Well, not as far as I know." He shrugs. "It's just the books. They seem to be more alive here than anywhere else."

"Halloween," I mutter as he shelves items in some indecipherable form of organization. "Magic's at its strongest, especially in Honeycrisp Hill. In two weeks, everything'll be normal again."

"It's more than that. I think there's something in this place . . ." Ian doesn't finish as Kal comes down the stairs. He offers to make us some tea instead, which I politely decline, though Kal very curtly says no.

Kal takes a seat on another box, twiddling her thumbs. I have the distinct impression that even though we saw each other only an hour ago, that was enough time for her to reconsider everything.

"Right. So . . . magic." I run my hands down my dress. "Huge world of magic. We did the easy spell. Wanna try that again?"

She looks around at all the boxes and at Ian, who's meandering his way to the kitchen, humming some jaunty little tune. She seems uncomfortable, and the way she looks at Ian makes me think she's not a fan of him and doesn't want to be here right now. I wonder why. But then, we don't know each other all that well yet. Maybe she'll tell me in time.

I make an instant decision. "What if we head back to the bakeshop? There's loads of magic there, magic you can touch, and maybe that'll be easier?"

Kal perks up right away. "Okay."

Now for the important part. "You can bring some of your family spellbooks, just in case, if you want."

"Already grabbed a few from upstairs earlier." She zips her worn, leather jacket that has a red patch on her elbow. When she sees me watching, the corner of her mouth lifts. "It's my dad's. He was into punk and moshing, all that." She lifts her bag from the floor and slings it across her shoulder.

We step outside, the warmth on my back instantly smoothing out my shivers. Why is it so much warmer outside than inside an old bookstore, even with a fire blazing?

The rainy chill from earlier feels like a lifetime ago as the autumn sun beats down on us. The air carries the scent of everything I love most about this season— pumpkins, apple cider brewed from Ada and Loretta's orchard, hay rides, cinnamon, the promise of more rain to come, and somewhere beneath it all, magic thrumming to life. I wish it could be fall all the time.

Or, really, I just wish I could eat a dozen apple cider doughnuts while reading a good book and watching the rain fall outside my attic bedroom window. But here I am, teaching and making conversation.

I decide to fill in the gaps of the conversation. "My dad's mostly into Broadway musicals, Motown, anything old and classic."

She shuts the door behind her, the bells jingling gently. "Seems like you are, too."

"True." I chuckle, glancing at my vintage dress. As we step onto the sidewalk, a car with blacked-out windows drives by, two flags waving on the front as if there's an important diplomat inside. There's not, though. It's the woman from before. The Enchantment Agency.

My stomach drops.

The wickedness. The cold. My spell. It's going to ruin everything.

"What's wrong?" Kal tugs at my arm, stares into my wide eyes. "You look sick."

"N-nothing," I stutter.

"Hey, isn't that the flag on the book Ms. Baird gave me? The lawbook?" Kal's head tilts to the side. "The Enchantment Agency, right? I swear they're everywhere."

"Mm-hmm," I hum airily.

"Right." She shrugs. "Is it normal that they came to town? I mean, I haven't seen too much wickedness or whatever."

I have, my mind screams, panic dulling my senses. "Let's get going. Um . . . the bakery—" My family bakery that's sinking under debt while the Enchantment Agency has come to town to accuse me of witchcraft. I'll just tell them I tweaked the spell, that I didn't know you can't create magic without a foundation. They'll understand. Maybe it has nothing to do with me.

It has nothing to do with me.

I'm building this whole thing up in my head for no reason. It's stress. Just stress. I'm afraid of change is all. Afraid Dad has been going to the bank or the real estate office to sell the bakery and that's where he was the other day.

Afraid I'll never get my chance to live up to Grandma Bernice and her greatness.

Afraid that without baking, I'll have nothing.

I let out a long sigh and set it all aside in my brain.

They're not here for me. Maybe someone else called a wickedness to town. I'm probably making a huge deal out of nothing. They're asking about my family because Coraline went bad, that's it. Nothing else.

"Uh, the bakery . . . You didn't finish what you were saying?" Kal cocks a brow.

"Sorry, yeah, lost my thought. Anyway, come on." I jerk my head in the direction of home. "Let's make magic."

Once we're in the courtyard behind the bakery, sitting at the old picnic table, I look her up and down.

"So, tell me, Kaliope Clarke: What are you waiting for?"

Kal stares at me with her brow furrowed, books strewn across the table. "What do you mean?"

My chest hitches; people tend not to like my honesty. But I plow forward anyway. "You've been an enchanter your entire life and you've never tried it before? You never went in search of these books on your shelves and tried to read them? Tried to teach yourself?" I quirk the corner of my lips. "It seems like you're waiting for something."

A next-door neighbor chooses that time to beat a rug from their second-floor balcony, cutting off what she was going to say in response. I shout hello, but only silence greets me. Typical.

Kal waits till they're finished before continuing. "My dad told me I couldn't practice magic without an education, that I'd mess up and end up hating it. That he knew people who had never gone to enchantment school, and because of that, they either refused magic altogether, or worse, they self-taught and ended up breaking laws they didn't know existed, which landed them in magic jail or something."

I chuckle. "Sounds fake."

Kal sniffs. "That's what he told me. He wouldn't lie to me."

"I'm not saying he's a liar." I sober quickly before I

offend her again. "I'm just saying, everyone has to learn and make mistakes along the way, school or no school, and they only toss people in magic jail when they screw up big-time." I didn't screw up, right? Right? I didn't mean to do witchcraft, and I probably didn't. I think. "Don't you feel good when you do magic? Doesn't it feel right?"

"Yeah," she admits.

I shake my head, splaying my fingers on the table. "I'm surprised is all, 'cause you look like a rebel in a leather jacket but you're so . . . obedient."

"Whatever." Her voice sounds small. "You said you'd teach me, not be a jerk."

I lean in closer. "I'm going to teach you, but you have to want to learn. You're going to have to push yourself. You said in school that you think you could be great at it, but greatness requires time and effort, and it's frustrating. If you want to be great, be prepared to fail."

She tosses her brown hair in the sunlight, and I catch glints of red in it. "I've already failed once."

"How?" My cheeks warm in the late-afternoon sun. "I thought you said you did the food part of your first spell right?"

"I did, but I tried to change a few things. The color of a tablecloth, the shape of a glass, tea to a muffin. Only the tea transformed to a muffin."

I shake my head. "Girl, you didn't fail. That's amazing,

food is usually the hardest to change." I pat her shoulder once. "Any spell that does something, even if it's not a hundred percent right, is a success. It means your magic works, you just gotta keep at it."

Her eyes narrow. "Really?"

I wave a hand. "You're going to do great."

A look of relief washes over her face, and I think I understand Kaliope Clarke. She's vulnerable, rule-abiding, cautious. And lonely. It's that last part that makes me want to hug her. She looks like she needs a good hug.

"You want to work at it . . . together?" The way she asks makes my heart beat a little faster.

"Together."

Something passes over her eyes, but then she smiles. "Let's do it."

12

Kal

It's raining again. Normally I find the rain pitter-pattering against the windows relaxing but even that doesn't stop the thoughts streaming in my mind right now.

Dad scrambles to shut off the beeping sound coming from the microwave upstairs while I stare out at the rain through the bookstore window. Though most of the books found homes on the shelves, there are still plenty left in stacks, waiting to be sorted. I shift in my high-backed cushion chair and yawn, journal in hand, wishing I could heat up my cold toes stuffed into fuzzy panda socks.

I've completed my super-important reflections on my mental health for the day—the act of writing about my state of being is supposed to make me feel better. And as much as I want to disagree, it works. Jenny would be proud. Hopefully the new therapist will be, too.

Jenny used to tell me anxiety doesn't just go away with a change of location and a new family dynamic—if anything, it could make it worse until it gets better. But being aware of that and documenting it is a positive step forward for my health. *Your health,* she'd say in her very calm, non-judgy tone, *is the one thing you can actively try to improve.*

Anxiety upended my whole world, but it's just a part of who I am. It's normal. Jenny told me to repeat that as often as I can. IT'S NORMAL.

I set my pen and journal down on the circular side table, the fire flickering on the metal lip, and take a sip of the blackberry tea that was in the box Wini gave us.

I'm so glad we found this place. I'm so glad Dad and I are here. I won't be so lonely anymore. I'm learning magic. I made a friend. I've got Violet. I'm beginning to feel whole here, like this is where I was meant to be. Things are going to be different for us, we're going to be a family.

Ian decides this, of all moments, is the right time to make his reappearance. He looks haggard, but there's a light in his eyes that wasn't there before. He takes another of the emerald-green high-backed chairs that were already here when we moved in and looks back over his shoulder to ask my dad, "How did you find this place?"

My dad sets down a plate of sandwiches on the small coffee table before taking a seat on the worn chocolate-brown leather couch opposite the fireplace.

"Remember when I investigated that story about the man who swerved off the road into a ditch filled with logs that somehow caught on fire and he was saved by a band of stray dogs called the Barkstreet Boys?"

I nod. Who could forget a story like that?

"That whole thing took place in Honeycrisp Hill."

The teacup warms my fingertips as I take another sip.

"While I was working the story, I took a look around town," Dad continues, his feet tapping the floor. "I saw this store and I guess I could never forget it." He looks wistfully at the fire dancing as if he sees the past in the flames. "I kept tabs on it, waiting for the price to drop. And when it did, I took off early in the morning to scope it out. Get a feel for it."

I set my sandwich down on the saucer of my empty teacup. "You never told me you came down here to check out Honeycrisp Hill."

"I didn't want you to get your hopes up." He glances at me. "If it didn't work out, then what?"

I try to keep the frustration from my voice. "How many times did you come down here?"

"About five or six. Whenever work slowed down and I could afford the gas."

And just like that, the moment is ruined.

I push to my feet, anger threading my words. "And

you didn't take me with you? Show me this world of enchantment?"

"Kal, it's not—"

"We barely saw each other outside of quick dinners for months, years! You never took me anywhere, said we couldn't afford it. All this time." My eyes fill with tears and I hate myself for them. The last thing I want to do is cry but that's just what happens when I'm this angry. "You left me *alone*."

"Kal—"

I don't hear the rest of the words as I walk up the stairs to our apartment, shutting the door behind me. I glance around, trying to catch my breath and let my anger fade. This place is way bigger than our home back in Boston. On my right there's a nice big kitchen, complete with a grand dining table with hardback chairs on one side and a church-like pew on the other.

There's a book on the table. It's tattered from reading it a million times . . . *A Wrinkle in Time*. Our favorite book. We'd highlight passages that meant the world to us while we were reading it, and leave Post-it notes to each other inside the pages. We'd write about the writing, mostly fangirling, sometimes to express something when we couldn't find the right words. Lately, over the past year, Dad would leave an apology in there for me when he missed something he said he'd be at, like

my choir concerts or art nights. It's how we communi-
cated.

I open the pages now, a note falling out by my feet. The
note feels warm, as if he'd just written it and magically
transported it into the book a few moments before. Maybe
he did.

Kal, I'm so sorry. Can you forgive me?

A sigh escapes through my teeth, and with it goes my
anger. I shut the book and put it on the table, clutching
the note in my hand.

I tread into my room and close the door behind me. I
sink onto the warm mattress and slide under the fluffy
purple blankets. The last thing I should do is go to bed in
my day clothes again. My therapist told me it's important to change my clothes to differentiate the stage of my
day. But I'm worn out.

"*Kaliope,*" a voice whispers through the door. "*Will
you speak with me?*"

Even Violet isn't enough to get me out of bed now. "I
can't," I say softly.

"*Adults are only happy when you follow their rules. When
you learn and live on their schedule.*"

"You've got that right." I sink farther into the mattress,
tugging every blanket I can find over my head, even the
weighted one that feels like a million pounds. I was silly
to think things were changing for Dad and me. Silly

to think we'd become a super-awesome family with no secrets, only joy and love.

"Remember, Kaliope"—Violet's voice is strong, unlike how I feel—*"you are more powerful than all of them."*

For the first time in a long time, I instantly fall asleep. I dream of a cold, cold room, where the walls are white and covered in ice.

There's a bed pushed against the far corner, a girl lying on top of it. All I can see of her is black straw-like hair, translucent skin, and the straps of a brown dress beneath a wool blanket. I creep toward the bed, reaching to wake her or touch her cheek, I don't know which.

As her eyes flicker open, my bare feet freeze in place. I open my mouth to scream but nothing comes out. Black ink oozes down the white walls, melting the ice and obscuring the light. It travels up my feet, down my fingertips; drops splash on my face.

I wipe it away just in time to see the girl bolt up from her bed, stopping an inch from my face.

Her black, bottomless eyes peer into my soul. "You shouldn't be here," she says, her voice a combination of different voices, both familiar and strange. And then I'm thrust back into reality, into my own bed, where there's color and warmth and my feet can move.

I clutch my comforter tighter around me, struggling to catch my breath. My skin prickles with goose bumps. My eyes dart around the room, landing on the foggy windowsill where *The Once Wicked* leans.

"Violet?" I ask, hoping she's awake. I need a friend to tell me everything's okay.

"Kal." Her voice is groggy, as if she was in a deep slumber, unlike me. *"What's wrong?"*

"It's nothing," I respond, not wishing to bother her. "Just a nightmare." A nightmare so detailed I almost believed it was real. A nightmare already fading in my mind. Still, I can't possibly go back to sleep.

"How old are you?" I cross the room, gently taking Violet's book in hand and then propping it on the pillow.

"When I was exiled? Oh, a bit older than you, I suppose. Thirteen. My thirteenth birthday, no less." Violet's voice is softer when she's being honest, something I've picked up on during the past few days.

"Why on your birthday?" I ask. I drag the elastic out of my hair and let it fan around me on the pillowcase.

"The magic within you declares itself, I'm sure you know . . . When you're thirteen you're finally allowed to use Level Nine magic and you can do all the spells on your own. Is that not why you moved here?" Her voice hitches, and in it I think I hear concern.

"No, we moved here because Dad wanted to. Has nothing to do with me." The words drip bitterly from my lips, and I don't apologize. I'm upset and I'm not sure when I won't be.

A wind howls outside, rattling the attic window and smoothing over my anger. A cool breeze drifts in, though I don't recall leaving the window open.

"Oh," Violet replies gently. "Well, *when you're thirteen, you're tested. The Agency decides what classes and training you'll need next, if you'll go to a special school or if you should have your magic stripped away—especially if your magic fits outside the scope of what they deem legal or normal. Magic that's not like everyone else in your family . . . they might consider that witchcraft. They believe it's like a wickedness within the heart of your magic. And then they exile you . . ."*

My eyebrows knit together. "'They' are the Enchantment Agency, right? Who are they really? We met someone who works there."

"*The Enchantment Agency regulates magic, like officers of the law. You have their book, don't you? They dole out punishment as judge, jury, and executioner. Read it, and you'll know their absolute power. Read it, and you'll know to be afraid.*"

A few beats of silence dangle between us. My mind thinks up a million questions as my eyes stare at the ceiling dotted with constellations of glow-in-the-dark stars I put up the first night here. I linger on Pisces, my astrological sign, which always reminds me of a fishing pole.

"Only something very . . . bad warrants their presence. Like when enchanters do magic without a foundation, they call it witchcraft."

"Oh," is all I can say. Another cool breeze floats in from the window and I savor the scent of fallen leaves coated in fresh rain that comes with it. I sit up, dread sinking into the pit of my stomach. "Is that how you ended up in a book? The Enchantment Agency punished you?"

"They thought I could be a witch." The friendly dullness is back in her tone, but I don't press her on it. "Not all magic is clear and simple. Defined. If you are different, if you contain magic that you shouldn't have, that hasn't been passed down to you, the Agency punishes you. That is how I ended up here." She sounds so emotionless, but I suddenly wish I could see her, to read her face, to know how she feels and what she's thinking. To have been deemed different and then punished doesn't seem fair. She lost everything. The chance to grow up, see her family, go to school, hang out with her friends . . . everything.

I imagine how I'd feel if I was taken away from Dad. Never see or hear from him again. Something in me shifts, something I don't want to think about at all. I shake my head, clearing the thought. "How long have you been inside that book?"

"I do not know the exact date, but it's been a very long

time. I've learned from each person who has come into the store. I've learned stories and dialects . . . Why, my best friend was none other than Coraline Mosley, who I suspect is your friend's mother. She taught me new magic and I taught her old magic."

I perk up. "She cursed the town, right?"

"The town had issues long before Coraline. It only worsened after her." There's a hesitance in Violet's words that pulls at the edges of my mind. She's hiding something and I want to know what.

I choose my next words carefully as my fingers run against the smooth comforter beneath me. Sleep is far from my mind at the moment. "What did, what does, the Agency want?"

Violet sighs. "Please, I must ask you not to ask me more about them. I've been in this book for longer than I lived outside of it. I have missed the world and the air. The food, how I miss food."

I laugh, my fingertips trailing the edge of my silk pillowcase. "I baked with Wini today. I got to help make the tastiest, most delicious things." With the subject changed to happier, more joyful things, my eyes begin to blink slower and slower. "Wini Mosley's my best friend."

"How do you know she's not using you?" Violet asks.

My eyes snap open once more. Suddenly I feel so, so cold. "What?"

"I *didn't say anything* . . ." Violet sighs. "*Are you all right?*"

"Cold," I mutter. "Just cold."

I get up and walk over to the window, trying to shut out the cool breeze that has suddenly dropped the temperature, but am surprised to find it's already shut. I press my palm to the glass, finding it decidedly warmer than the air circulating my room. My brows knit together. I imagine it's probably just my mind playing tricks on me. Maybe it's always been cold and I'm only noticing it now.

I bounce back onto the bed and slip beneath the covers, Violet's book propped up beside me.

Recipe Journal of Winifred Mosley

MY "SHOULD-BE-FAMOUS" HOT COCOA

Straight up, this is the best hot chocolate recipe in the history of the world. As judged by me, and I'm the only one who can accurately judge hot chocolate as I've had it every day since I was four. I'm not saying I have an addiction, but I am saying that my body runs on hot chocolate.

Ingredients:

85 grams of a Lindt (or another good-quality, low-sugar) milk chocolate bar

100 grams semisweet chocolate (this can be lower quality)

1/2 cup cocoa powder (adjust this based on how dark/rich you want your mixture; I used a mixture of super-dark cocoa and regular)

1/2 cup granulated sugar (adjust this based on how sweet you like your hot cocoa)

1 tablespoon cornstarch

Pinch of sea salt (a generous 1/8 teaspoon)

For one serving:

2 cups milk (my favorite is oat milk but you can use whatever you want!)

4-5 tablespoons chocolate mixture

How to make:

1. This recipe will require a food processor OR you can grate the chocolate. I've had to grate the chocolate for this, and it takes FOREVER. But if you put on a Netflix show or . . . I don't know, your favorite podcast about the secret lives of gnomes (don't laugh, I've heard they're very scandalous) at least you'll be entertained.

2. Combine all the dry ingredients in a processor and mix until sandy appearance. OR if you had to grate the chocolate, combine with sifted cocoa powder, cornstarch, sugar, and salt. Mix with a whisk.

3. Put the chocolate mixture in a sealable bag.

4. Heat the 2 cups milk on the stove in a small saucepan. Add 4-5 tablespoons of the mixture. This is all personal preference! Add however much you like based on taste. You'll have enough mixture for 7-10 servings.

5. As always, ENJOY. Don't drink all the mixture in one day, though. It can result in unnecessarily loud laughter, jitteriness, and excess energy followed by extreme lethargy. Yes, I learned this from personal experience.

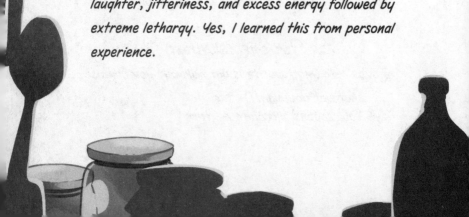

13

Wini

After school, we're sitting at the picnic table behind the bakery again, practicing spells while the afternoon sun shimmers behind the trees.

The air streaming from the propped-open door to the bakeshop makes my stomach growl. Maddie's baking brown butter sugar cookies. Brown butter has a very distinct nutty scent that lingers in my nose and swirls around me in a haze of deliciousness, threatening to pull me inside like a lasso. I try to shake the thought away as I turn to Kal, who's nestled in a bright red blanket, sipping from her steaming cup of apple cider on the bench beside me, her back against the table. Her mouth's pulled into a perfect frown.

I scoot over, trying to not ruin the vibe I've got from the scent of brown butter and the cinnamon stick in my own cup of apple cider. I'm really trying to cut back on hot chocolate. Five cups a day feels like it's getting out of hand.

Kal sighs. "We've been at this all day and I can't manage *one* word enchantment spell. Watch." She sits up, setting her drink aside, and picks up a yellow leaf that's browning at the edges. Her voice dips into the singsongy tone of a word enchanter, the great orators of the enchantment world. "The yellow leaf fell from the deep, dark woods behind the bakery onto the ground before me, Kaliope Clarke. I pick it up gently by its stem and whisper, *Bend up toward the sky and fly back to your tree, little leaf.*"

The leaf doesn't even shake in the slight breeze. It just stands there before her, unwavering, not ready to acquiesce to her demands at all. That's how word enchantment is supposed to work. The enchanter says small phrases like a writer, speaking a story into existence. They can make things move. They can make words leap off pages into someone's mind like a movie. They are the best authors in the world. The more power and experience, the longer the story they can make come true.

Kal, sadly, doesn't have the touch. Yet.

I grimace. "Maybe I'm a bad teacher . . ."

"No." Kal nudges me with her shoulder, her usually bright face downcast. "It's not you. It's me."

"Good, because I feel like I'm an *amazing* teacher." I laugh, and I'm happy to see her grin just a little. "Have you ever considered that maybe you should ask your dad or grandpa for help? I mean, I know I'm great, but I'm not a word enchanter. I do food. It's in my blood. Words won't work for me."

"I don't want to. It's not . . ." She trails off, reaching for her cup and gripping it tight.

"You're stalling. I think you're embarrassed by failing at spells so you won't ask for help, Kaliope." I drag her name out slowly.

She looks at the ground, her cheeks a rosy red. "I'm not stalling. And it's not that I'm embarrassed—"

"Oh it's definitely that you're embarrassed. You expect too much of yourself. And you can't just start enchanting and not screw it up. Everyone messes up the first, second, even third time." My head falls back and I stare up into the pale blue sky that's darkening at the edges. "The first time I tried to make enchanted brownies, I made rocks. Chocolate stones. If you threw one, you could break a window. It was an epic fail."

"Really?"

"Really. Grandma Bernice laughed and laughed and laughed. Said she made a baguette that tasted like sawdust the first time. Dad made a cake that burst like a balloon when you cut into it. Maddie's Chantilly cream turned into water after just a few seconds."

There's a ghost of a smile on Kal's face. "And then you tried again and it worked?"

Now it's my turn to laugh. "No! You just keep trying

until it works. You learn as much as you can, and then you do it. I needed to learn the actual ingredients to brownies. I needed to know how to make them, what they should look and taste like. The fifth time was the charm. There's a saying for the Mosleys: *If at first you don't succeed, try it again four more times.*

Kal blinks slowly, her body falling forward, and I sit up. "Hey, I'm sorry. What did I say?"

She mashes her lips together. "I've tried some of these word spells hundreds of times. At night before bed. In the morning while I'm brushing my teeth. Maybe I just don't have it." She closes her eyes and runs a hand over her forehead.

"You know what you need?" The realization slams into me like a rolling pin into cold butter. "A change of pace. Come into the bakeshop again. I'll teach you some more baking. If your mind's distracted, maybe you'll have a breakthrough."

"I don't see how that's going to help me," she mutters. "Besides, we still haven't even begun working on our school project."

"O ye of little faith, *this* is the project. But . . ."—I try to keep the excitement from my tone—"if you want a challenge, I do have a spell we could re-create . . . if you're interested."

Kal shrugs, and I'll accept it as interest because if we

can pull it off, it'll be the biggest and best spell of all time. It'll save Wayward Sentiments and send all the shadows and witches back to where they came from.

"I tried an experimental love spell before you arrived, and it failed, big-time. So if we put our heads together, do some research, we can tweak the spell, and it'll be amazing." I don't say that it could be considered witchcraft, that it might've set some weird things in motion in town and brought the Enchantment Agency to investigate, and that it'd probably be deemed illegal. She doesn't really need to know that. In fact, it's safer that she doesn't.

"A love spell? Like capital *L Love?*" Kal frowns. "The emotion?"

"Yes," I continue. "Imagine if we could help people fall in love? It could change the world. People would be happy. Not . . . alone."

Kal taps her fingers against her cup. "Can we . . . Is that okay to do?"

"Of course it is," I lie again. "It's just a bit of enchantment."

Kal's head tilts to the side, brow furrowed. "How will it work?"

"Eh . . ." I collect my words, trying to say this the simplest way I can. "So my grandma, Bernice Mosley, wrote a grand love spell called An Enchanted Match. It's supposed to work by . . ."—*using someone's crush as a foundation so it won't be witchcraft*—"finding out what someone looks for in a partner, collecting important items that mean something to them, and then saying some words. It's easy, and packs a punch. We just need to tweak it to be more general."

For a moment, I think she's going to say no.

But then she smiles. "I like it. We should do it."

"Yes!" I smack her shoulder before hopping to my feet. "Now, do you want to sit out here as it gets cold and keep failing? Or do you want to come with me and eat some sugar cookies while we make garlic pinwheels and try something new?"

Kal looks around, shivering despite the blanket draped around her shoulders. She's so small, I wonder how she functions in this weather. I have all my glorious padding to keep me warm, whereas she looks like a slight breeze might blow her away. Her gaze catches mine and the corners of her lips quirk.

"How could I resist sugar cookies?"

I cock my eyebrow. "*Brown butter* sugar cookies."

Her brow furrows again as she takes my outstretched hand, letting me pull her to standing. "What's the difference?"

"Oh, Kal." I thread her arm through mine, casting a glance at the spellbooks we leave behind on the table. "You have so much to learn."

After we settle behind the bench, the front door jingles and there's someone at the counter. Maddie's too into her work to notice.

"Be right back." I straighten, putting on a serious face. I put a little charm in my voice as I sweep into the front of the house. "Hello, how can I help you today?"

"Well, dear," a woman with a strong voice says, "what do you have in this bakery that can cure a weak heart?"

I step up to the counter and try not to gasp. I've only seen her in passing but I know who this woman is. The agent.

"Uh." I falter, and I glance at Kal's face peeking out from behind the door. The customer's eyes dart to her and then back to me. She's in a long black dress, brown hair pulled back in a tight bun, and her piercing green eyes don't seem to miss anything. "When you say weak, do you mean medically, like a heart issue, or—"

"I mean someone who is too afraid to make the right decision because they fear breaking their heart." Her tone is authoritative and somewhat terrifying. Her lips twist at the corner as she watches me. "You look so much like your mother."

"My mother?" I ask, the words cracking a little. "You knew her?"

The woman only grins. "*Know* her."

"Really? You . . . know where she is?" There's a bit of

hope in my words and maybe even dread. On one hand, this woman's presence in my shop is not good. Not good at all. But the idea of Coraline being out there shifts my focus. Do I want to see Coraline Mosley after all this time? Do I want to meet the woman who nearly destroyed our town and abandoned me on her family's doorstep? Do I want to know if she regretted that decision—if she loved me, and it was an impossible choice? What would it even be like to have a mom?

"Sorry," is all the woman says with a shrug. Not a yes or a no. Not helpful at all. "Do you think you have something for the weak heart?"

I stay silent for a few beats before answering, my heart hammering. "I have Decisive Doughnuts on hand, though not too many. They're pumpkin with a cinnamon-apple glaze. Made fresh this morning . . ." I blabber on nervously.

Kal steps in, getting the woman's attention. "There's also Strong Sponge Cake. They're fluffy with a fresh cream and the first clementines of the season."

I toss her a look that tells her I'm grateful for the help.

"How about both?" the woman says with a big smile that stretches her black-lipsticked lips. Very few people can pull that color off, but she does.

My hands shake as I try to box up the desserts. I take off to grab the bakery logo sticker, leaving Kal with that terrifying force of nature. Thankfully the bakeshop is small so I can overhear them.

"Kaliope, right?"

Kal nods. "You're the lady we met outside of town, aren't you? The one who's watching my grandpa and trying to find out who called a wickedness to Honeycrisp Hill."

The woman laughs—well, more like cackles. "Figures a Clarke would find the strongest enchanter in town to teach her magic. The two of you together . . . why, you'd be the envy, maybe even the target, of every coven in the country."

Kal starts to ramble just like I did. "I thought only witches do covens? Although it sounds cool if enchanters do it, and I would totally love to dress like one of those old-timey characters in cartoons."

I emerge from the back, somewhat exasperated, as I close the box and slide it onto the counter. "That'll be $8.50." My voice wobbles, but I make myself stand straighter.

"Keep the change. You need it." The woman pushes a twenty toward me and my lip instinctively curls. "I'm looking forward to . . . catching you around town."

"Catching?" I suddenly blurt. I shift on my feet, waiting to see if she's going to be honest or as vague as before. Did she say *catching* because she knows it was me who cast the wayward spell?

She smiles. "My name's Esmerelda Diaz, head witch hunter of the Enchantment Agency. You may not have heard of me, but I've heard of you. *Both* of you."

She's trying to intimidate me into confessing. But I won't.

"You've heard of me? Why?" I chuckle, trying to cover up the panic spreading through my gut. "I just make pastries all day. Although they *are* pretty delicious, if I do say so myself."

Esmerelda doesn't look amused. "You're the daughter of one of the wickedest witches in history." My mouth drops open but before I can reply, she continues. "And she"—she points at Kal—"is the granddaughter of Ian Clarke, one of the best witch hunters there ever was—until he up and quit. It was all very . . . *suspicious*."

Kal and I exchange a quick glance, both speechless.

"Someone summoned a wickedness to this town. It seems *someone* is continuing an old spell that was better left alone." She pauses, eyeing us both. I can feel sweat sliding down my back. "I *will* find the culprit." She gives us a smile before walking toward the door. "If it was you . . . or"—she twists around, her eyes pinning me in place—"you know who it was, confess now. Otherwise, this wickedness will continue. If we don't fix it in time, the whole town could be destroyed."

14

Kal

You *can do magic without needing a medium first, you know,"* Violet says as I brush my hair before school. She's the first person I speak to every morning, and there's something really reassuring about her presence. I've never felt more seen or heard before in my life, and I need that.

"Like the basic emotions spell Wini taught me?" I try to focus on the conversation as Della croons from my alarm clock radio. I put music on to add a little calm to my morning, but there's a knot of anxiety in the pit of my stomach. That Esmerelda Diaz lady freaked Wini out yesterday, which freaks me out since Wini is usually confident and collected. Something must be wrong, but I can't imagine what. And Wini wouldn't say.

"Exactly." Violet pierces my thoughts. *"Do you want to know another basic spell?"*

I set the brush down and I pull my sweater tighter around me. It's always so cold in this room. "Yes, please."

"There are many, but my favorite one is to stop time for a few moments. Enchanters use this spell often. It helps to

understand a situation you might find yourself in or to fix a problem before it occurs." She pauses for a moment as if she's remembering times when she used the spell outside of her book. "Would you like to learn it?"

"Definitely." I step closer to the windowsill, the chill creeping through my sweater even more now.

"It's very easy. It goes: Ticktock, goes the clock. One to minute, one to hour, stop them both with my power." She says it rhythmically, and the words wash over me.

"When you do spells, they don't work, do they?" I look around the room, trying to sense if the spell took effect and made time stop. But my alarm clock is still ticking away, Della is still bopping, and I'm not frozen.

"No, I'm in a book. Spells don't work for me anymore," she says it matter-of-factly, but I sense an edge of frustration in her tone. "Do you want to try it? It won't last long, but the better you get at it, the longer you will have stopped time."

"Okay . . ." I close my eyes and clear my head. "Ticktock, goes the clock. One to minute, one to hour, stop them both with my power."

There's a whoosh of air and then a sudden stillness in my room. Little specks of dust floating in the morning light halt in midair like suspended stars. It's so . . . quiet. I walk around, bending down to my alarm clock, which sits silent. The numbers don't move and there's no Della.

My mouth drops open. Wow. Now that's magic. Fast-acting, truly powerful magic.

The air whooshes again and the dust falls, Della sings, and the clock ticks.

"Did it work?" Violet asks quickly.

I smile, though I know she can't see me. "Yeah, I think it did! How cool is that?!" I nearly screech this time while jumping up and down. Many of the spells I've tried haven't worked and those that did I had to repeat several times. This one worked right away. I smile wider.

Violet joins in with my excitement. *"You are truly on your way to becoming a great enchanter, Kaliope Clarke."*

I laugh. "Maybe I am. Wanna teach me some more tonight?"

"I would love to," she says quietly. *"You're a good student and I have many wonderful spells you can do."*

I keep that joy with me all the way through school and even into the bakeshop later. Wini teaches me to make bread with chunks of cheddar, roasted red pepper, and garlic. She's on edge—though she says she's not—and has been giving me tons of little spells to practice while I knead the dough. She says that if I concentrate on what my hands are doing, I won't trip up and over-whelm myself with magic.

She's right. And as it turns out, I love baking. Who would've thought I'd love making food as much as I love eating it? Even better, it seems to put my anxiety at ease. I mean, it's still there, but I can't really focus on it when my hands and brain are so busy.

Baking feels right. In my soul. Like it's a part of me I didn't know existed until my hands are caked with dough and flour and I'm weighing butter on a digital scale. Today is a really good day.

"See those little flaps of dough that aren't as smooth as the rest?" Wini holds her bowl of cookie dough that smells like chocolate and brown sugar. Her rainbow polka-dot apron matches her bandanna, and her red glasses glimmer.

"Yeah?" I ask, smearing a bit of flour across my brow with my arm.

She picks up the metal cookie scoop, her pink lips lifting at the edges. Where did she even find gloss that bright? "Tuck them under, pinch them, and then keep rolling, okay?"

"Yup." I do as she says, my elbow hitting the wicker proofing bowl. I've been in here every day after school and therapy for three days, and I've never felt more at home.

"Don't forget to do the spell." Wini has me writing my own spells, learning how to phrase them like all word enchanters do. I'm getting the hang of it. My word spells don't work, but basic ones and foodie ones seem to go off without a hitch. Actually, I'm sort of proud of how well I'm doing at the foodie spells.

She plops perfect balls of dough on the sheet pan and then dots them with yellow drops of essence she calls Focus. That's another thing I've learned: Focus falls under the umbrella of Confidence, Calm is blue, Love is purple, Anger is orange, Sadness is red, Worry is green, and Happiness is a rainbow . . . which I found especially weird since those feelings aren't all good. But Wini assured me, to be happy, truly happy, you have to feel everything else.

My nose scrunches as I consider my words carefully. *"With my hand and magic command, this dough to rise before my eyes."*

Once the words leave my tongue, the dough rises gently in the bowl, nice and puffy. Perfect!

"Extraordinary." Wini grins, shoving the sheet pan on a rack to be baked. "Auntie," she calls out to Maddie, who's behind the counter. "Look what she can do. Have you ever seen anything like it? From someone whose medium isn't food?"

I stare at her. "What do you mean?"

"We can't do magic like yours without a cost. If I tried a word spell—you know, the kind your family does with all the flowery language, that doesn't need to rhyme—"

"A loaf of bread takes two hours to rise," Maddie cuts

in. "It takes energy. When we do a spell like that, it's pulling at the very foundation of our magic. But for you, it should take that energy. Your magic should be depleted. Enchantment using a medium that's not your own can't come from nothing. You can't create from nothing."

I shift on my feet, my boots sinking into the black fatigue mat. "How do you know that it didn't do that to me? Isn't that dangerous?"

"I had a feeling it would work, and I was watching you the entire time. If it affected you, I would have noticed." Wini shrugs.

I shake my head. "That's mean, you know that, right?"

Maddie frowns, putting her hand on her hip and tipping her head to the side. "Winifred, you didn't tell her what could happen?"

"I started off with a teeny spell and went from there to see how far we could go! Kal's got talent we haven't seen before from word enchanters. She's like us." She waves her hands excitedly. "I'm proud of you, Kal." She glances at Maddie. "I'm sorry I didn't tell you."

I only nod, keeping my own excitement inside. What could that mean? I wonder if Dad would be impressed? Maybe not everything's as bad or as lonely and hopeless as I sometimes think.

"The girl's got a gift, all right." Maddie leans against the door. "Sure you're not a food enchanter?"

My cheeks pink, or at least they feel warmer than before. I've never gotten so many compliments in my life, and especially not on my enchanting. It's everything I ever wanted. I run my sweaty fingers down my apron to contain my pride. "Aren't mediums genetic? Don't I have to be a word enchanter?"

"Not always," Maddie says, looking away. She unties her apron, setting it against the radio. "Magic is never a set thing. Although, if an enchanter has another type of magic, it can lead to trouble. They say those with a different type of . . . uninherited magic are dangerous. Magic from nothing is dangerous." Maddie tosses me a look, and then her face softens. "Don't worry. Sometimes people learn their medium best when they practice another. You'll be fine."

Still, I think about Violet. She said the Enchantment Agency thinks those who have uninherited magic are witches. That they considered *her* a witch. What if I'm like that? Would I be exiled, too?

"She could be a food enchanter though, right?" I'm surprised Wini isn't grimacing at the implication of me having the same magic as her.

"Mm-hmm . . . Did you work on your school project? What spell have you come up with?" Maddie pins us both with a glare.

"Well," Wini says slowly, and I know where she's going

with this. We've been discussing it all week, research-ing it every spare moment using Clarke grimoires. "We want to fix one of Grandma's experimental spells. If it works, we could keep the business afloat and impact people in a positive way."

"I don't think that's a good idea." Maddie bunches her lips together in thought. "Kal may be able to do food spells without draining her energy, but Mama's spells require a dangerous use of power. Power far beyond the two of you, beyond even her or Cora—Why not try something from one of our family's grimoires, something fun? Like dancing spells or something?"

"Okay," Wini and I mutter at the same time. Seems like everyone wants the world to be better, but there are so many rules that prevent it. It's just like Violet said. People are only happy when you learn what they want on their schedule. Still though, if Maddie thinks it's dangerous, why didn't Wini say so?

"Also, maybe don't tell anyone, even Ms. Baird, about Kal's magic just yet, okay? Give it time to sort itself out." Maddie pats us both on the arms. "You girls got the shop? There's an emergency meeting about the weird things that have been happening around town."

Wini exhales loudly. "Weird things? Like the shad-ows and you know . . . I don't know, the sudden stormi-ness . . . or . . . has more happened or gotten worse?"

Hm, even I seem to know more about this than Wini. "Everyone at school was whispering about magic being on the fritz. Spells aren't working like they're supposed to, lights keep blinking out, it's stormy, *and* there are shadows." Not to mention the strange coldness that's been hanging around, especially in my room, though I don't tell them that.

"Well, I guess I didn't hear the rumors." Wini shrugs casually but it looks stiff even to me.

"That's 'cause you have selective listening skills." Maddie's gaze narrows on Wini. "Anyway, nothing you two need to concern yourselves about. The adults will figure it all out. The Enchantment Agency is here to help." She flicks us both one last look. "You got the store though, right?"

"Yeah, sure." Wini shrugs, though I see her hands shake by her sides.

"I think she's beginning to like me," I say, as Maddie slips up the stairs and out of sight.

Wini shakes her head. Her voice sounds a bit off. "Weird, right? She still doesn't like me and she *raised* me."

I laugh, stepping over to the sink to scrub the dough from my fingers. If I've learned anything over at the bakery, it's that dough has a way of getting on everything. "Maybe it's because I'm more charming than you."

"Don't be ridiculous," Wini huffs, lips pursed, head

shaking, the strangeness from before gone. "I'm extremely charming, some even say enchanting."

"Who says that?" I cock an eyebrow as my foot plonks on the pedal to turn the water on.

Wini grins. "It doesn't matter. I've just heard it, that's all you need to know."

The water's hot and soothing enough to coax the stickiness away. "So . . . when were you going to tell me about the spell being too dangerous for us?"

Wini inhales sharply, turning toward me. "Maddie thinks any spell that's not basic is dangerous. You don't see her doing a lot of magic because she's uptight about it."

"I learned a basic spell just today that allows you to stop time. If that's basic, then this love spell must be really serious." I put my hands on my hips, pinning Wini with a glare.

"There aren't spells to stop time," Wini says with a shake of her head. "And if there were, there's no way they'd be basic. There's no such thing as time enchanters."

I lift my eyebrows, ignoring the idea of Violet's spell not being basic. If it wasn't, how could I have done it on my first try? No, I'm not going to tell Wini about that. I'm going back to the original subject. "Are you telling me the truth about that love spell, Wini? Are we going to get into trouble for this?"

"No. It's harmless enchantment. Elementary, really,"

she says, her eyes boring into mine. In them, I see desperation, but I can't understand why.

I decide not to push it for now and instead offer levity. "Okay, Sherlock."

Wini grins. I've never had a best friend, but . . . sometimes, it feels like she could be it. "You just keep working on your magic. It's important you get good at it so we can do our spell."

"You got it, boss."

A few hours later, back in my room, Violet teaches me some more basic spells that I crush right away, giving me a confidence boost I so desperately need. I'm sprawled out on the braided carpet, feeling good—actually better than good—when Violet turns thoughtful.

"What is having anxiety like?" she asks me suddenly, throwing me off slightly.

My fingers drum against the carpet while I answer as honestly as I can. "I guess it's like having a voice in your head telling you about everything that could go wrong and will go wrong and how you aren't good at anything. It's like you're . . . you're always afraid. Always in a state of panic."

"Mm . . ." Violet sounds pensive. *"I can imagine that's exhausting."*

"Yeah, it is exhausting." I exhale in relief. It's nice when someone understands and cares. "But I'm getting better at finding my new normal and . . . learning how to live with it. I think the magic helps."

"Magic always helps, if only we had more of it." Before I can ask what she means, she goes on. *"I'm here for you, too, Kal. You and me, we're powerful together. And I just want to help you be happy and healthy."*

"Thanks, Violet. You are, I promise." I smile to myself, since I'm not sure she can see me. "Now what's next? I'm having too much fun learning."

That smile lingers as she tells me more about magic. For the first time in a long time, I don't feel like I'm sinking in the ocean. There are people and things keeping me afloat. Baking helps. Wini helps. But most of all, talking with Violet helps.

She is so . . . I don't know, but I trust her. She's kind and listens. She makes me feel less alone. She doesn't judge me about what I know or don't know and she's patient. I almost wish I could meet her.

Or maybe, somehow, I could free her from the book.

15
Wini

Ms. Baird's beehive is deflated today, and her red hair shines a little less brilliantly. When she picks up her cup of tea, she spills it all over herself. With a mumbled *excuse me*, she darts out of the classroom. Everyone begins to chitter.

"I heard she went to the town meeting last night and told everyone that she was taking a walk through the woods when she saw a ghost! A real ghost!" Jacob Lee slams his book down hard, getting everyone's attention. "Ghosts haven't been seen around here since . . ." He doesn't finish his thought, just glares at me.

Kal leans into me. "Wini, are there such things as ghosts?"

"Yeah," I say, arranging my spellbooks on my desk. "The only place believed to be haunted, though, is your bookstore, and I haven't seen a ghost there. Have you?"

She shakes her head. "But you know about them?"

"I mean, sure. Who doesn't, right?" Janet snarks with her friends. "You really are so new, I'm surprised they even let you in our class. They should've put you in with baby enchanters, the toddlers' group that meets on Monday mornings." She laughs and her friends cackle with her.

I give Janet a glare and she goes quiet. People may make fun of me all the time, calling me Betty Crocker and whatever, but they all agree I'm the most powerful enchanter in class. "Ghosts are dangerous, Kal. They're wicked."

Her brow furrows. "Why?"

"Because they can manipulate you, taste your magic, and use it for their own means. They like to play tricks and feed off emotions. The more power you give them, the more solid they become." I slip a spell for a paper airplane across the table. "We've read all about them. The only thing you need to know is that if you ever see one, you have to run." I clear my throat and the others get the hint to leave us alone. "Try this spell. It's really fun."

Kal studies it for a moment. "A paper airplane?"

"Yeah, you'll like it." I nod, trying to encourage her. The more confident she becomes, the better she'll learn. Besides, it's a nice distraction from ghosts, An Enchanted Match, the Enchantment Agency, or wicked things in town.

Kal attempts to make the paper airplane with a word spell, but the paper just sits there, flat in her hands. Her shoulders slump.

"It's Level Three magic. Even a *word* enchanter should be able do it," Janet says with a snide smile. Her medium is art. She can pick up a brush dabbed with paint and create a masterpiece with just a few words. Her mom is the town's portraitist. Janet flops a piece of paper onto her desk. "It's easy, watch." She looks down at it. *"Paper to fold, paper to plane, fly it high across the sky."*

The paper folds into the perfect airplane. It lifts off her desk evenly, and suddenly soars above the classroom . . . and combusts in a fiery ball over Daniella Badua's head. Daniella leaps from her seat with a squeak and points her finger at Janet.

"You did that on purpose! You . . . you . . . witch!"

Janet's eyes fill with tears. "I didn't! I'm not . . . I didn't mean to . . ." She throws her hands over her face and bolts out of the classroom. None of her so-called friends go after her.

I'm about to go find her myself and say something nice when there's a big *boom*! Glass shatters and the floor shakes. We all get out of our seats and run into the hallway where the upside-down table with the vase and flowers now lies in pieces all over the floor.

Ms. Baird has her arms wrapped around a wailing Janet. Both of them look ashen and terrified.

I step closer, finding the flowers that were once so

perfectly alive are now fading into dust that scatters in the wind.

"Class is canceled for the rest of the day." Ms. Baird's voice wobbles until she puts a little authority into it. "Be safe, everyone, and I still expect those"—her eyes catch on the splintered wood—"those spells, next week."

"Dad . . . What did Coraline do?"

We stop beside the statue in the town square. I glance up at Derrick, whom Mr. Collins must've wrapped a cashmere scarf around, and grip my hot chocolate tighter. I know I said I'd reduce my intake but how could I with Esmerelda Diaz lurking about, making me feel like a villain? Or watching Coraline's table shatter? Or seeing Janet's paper airplane burst into flames?

Dad sighs, his nostrils flaring slightly. I know people say I look like her, but in this moment, I feel every bit his daughter. "Coraline was—is—powerful." He pauses uncomfortably. He's never wanted to talk about this. Not the specifics. But I feel like I need to know, and I think he sees that.

I gulp the hot chocolate, nearly burning my throat. The wind howls as another thick breeze whips past us. The weather's been getting so unpredictable, even by

New England standards. There've been strong gales of freezing air up and down Main Street recently.

Despite the cool and stormy weather, nearly everyone's out and preparing for tomorrow night's jumble sale. The townsfolk get together and set up booths to sell antiques, books, and artwork. The whole event is candlelit, and sometimes folks dress up as crows for absolutely no reason at all. Our bakery will have a booth run by Aunt Maddie. I've been banned, since my presence seems to worsen our already terrible sales.

Despite the bustle, there's a bubble around us. There always is. No one waves or approaches for small talk.

"Coraline cast a spell to steal magic from every . . . from enchanters within the town limits. She set up barriers so that they couldn't escape." Dad stares at his feet, coffee in hand. "I don't know why she did it."

For a moment, I can't find the words. Another cold breeze nips at my cheeks and I step closer to him. "How did they know it was her?"

"The Enchantment Agency stepped in. They couldn't dissolve the barriers around the town, they said it was the strongest spell they'd ever seen, but they could return the stolen magic within the limits of the barrier. Before they could punish Coraline, she fled. They decided to curse her, using some of her hair and belongings, making it so that she could no longer come home. It was meant as a measure to keep her out of the enchanted world and stop her from conspiring with others. I guess while Coraline was responsible for the spell, she wasn't strong enough to pull it off by herself. They believed there was someone else in town that worked with her. They searched everywhere but couldn't find the culprit."

I swallow the lump threatening to block all airflow in my throat. "What would they have done to her . . . if they caught her, I mean?"

"I'm not sure." Dad inhales. "They would have stripped her magic, probably, and then sent her to jail."

Is that what Esmerelda Diaz will do to me if she finds out I might've mistakenly called a wickedness to town? I try not to shout over my pounding heart. "If they reversed her spell, why is the town still cursed?"

This time, he doesn't answer right away. His eyes shift to a passerby before falling on me, and he blows out a long breath. "I don't know." His words are hesitant. I can see how uncomfortable he is. "It's possible . . . whoever was working with her . . . The Agency thought removing Coraline's presence would remove the barriers and the effects of the spell. It didn't, and now, within the barriers, those touched by the curse are still not quite *whole*. It's possible—because of us, because her blood flows through us—that the spell can't be broken unless we leave."

I stare at him. So it's true. It *is* us. The whole town hates us for a reason. But if we leave, we lose our magic, too. There has to be another way.

"I didn't know. I'm sorry," I say, until his face turns a normal shade of brown.

"Don't." He holds a hand up. "Don't apologize. It's not your fault. And it's just . . . we don't *know* that's the reason. We don't know exactly what she did. I didn't . . . I didn't want you to worry about it. It's not like we had anywhere else to go, and . . ."

I can see the conflict on his face. Having to choose between abandoning everything our family had built and possibly saving the town, or letting everyone else continue to suffer from the curse's effects. I can also sort of understand why everyone would be angry we didn't even try.

The question that has been plaguing me since I opened Grandma Bernice's book finally breaks free and streams out like chocolate from a molten lava cake. "Dad, is Coraline . . . a wicked witch?"

"She was powerful, and rebellious in her beliefs. She didn't mind using wicked magic to reach her goals. But is she a witch?" He closes his eyes, his breath evening out. "I don't know. I've never seen a witch, but they have a bad reputation. What Coraline did . . . it's beyond words, and I hate that she did it. But I don't want to think the worst of her."

"I wish I could say the same." I take another sip of my hot chocolate, pulling my green trench coat tighter around me.

"I have faith that one day they'll let her come back home. They'll let her redeem herself." He says it wistfully, and I want to believe him.

I see Kal and Lachlan meander by us with ice creams in hand. It's got to be forty degrees out. Kal's leather jacket is even flapping open in the wind, while Lachlan's only wearing his tweed blazer with patches at the elbow.

"Hi." Lachlan smiles, and Dad's face lights up incandescently, brighter than the streetlamps that are flicking on.

"Hey, Lachlan. Hello, Kal." My dad's tone is no longer somber and full of regret but instead full of life and energy and hope.

Kal gives a small wave, peering around at the residents of Honeycrisp Hill as they do their shopping and moseying. I see Mr. Klein setting up his rickety wooden booth. One year he tried to sell a portrait of Vlad the Impaler with a little candleholder at the bottom, as if to honor or commemorate him—we're not sure. Unsurprisingly, no one bought it. The rumor is he's somehow related to the Prince of Darkness. The speculations are just as absurd as the portrait.

Honeycrisp Hill is a haven for weird people.

"So . . . how have you adjusted to Honeycrisp Hill? Do you like it here?" My dad steps closer to Lachlan, and Kal gets tense. She has that same look she did when they first met. It's like she doesn't want her dad talking to my dad, and for the life of me, I can't understand why.

Or . . . maybe I can. I get the impression that things aren't great at home for Kal.

"It's great. We love it," she answers for him. "Well, we just wanted to grab ice cream and head home . . ."

Lachlan throws a quick glance her way. "I do like it here. It's a lot to get used to, but it's the perfect place to settle down. I'm certain this will be our forever home. And the bookstore is coming along well. We'll open on Halloween. Are we still on for dinner?"

"We would love to," I say as someone who isn't currently in huge trouble for accidentally calling a wickedness, messing with her dad's love life, and possibly ruining the town. Yep, all good over here.

"Ah, yes, please," Dad responds with a big, cheesy smile. "Did you know about the downtown rule that we have to have candy for trick-or-treaters at our stores? For enchanter kids, they have to actually do a magic trick for you. The humans—" He continues rambling and Lachlan seems totally entranced.

I sidle up to Kal, leaning close to her ear. "What's your deal?"

She lets out a long breath. "You wouldn't understand."

"Try me," I whisper.

Her voice is edged with anger. "My dad's been nearly nonexistent in my life."

I furrow my brow, but then, I kind of suspected something like that. She's an enchanter who had been raised without magic and left on her own to figure it out. Well, until me. "So you want to punish him for it?"

She opens her mouth to respond, but then the weirdest thing happens.

One by one the people around us stop and turn. Their eyes glaze over and they seem to line up in formation. All we can do is stand and watch as our neighbors focus and then . . . they begin stomping their feet to a beat.

They make a weird collective noise, like twangy guitars. The town mechanic, Bill, who's an old Black man with a heavy dose of freckles speckled across his cheeks, steps up in front of everyone. He's in his blue jumpsuit with his name in red on the side and his black boots are covered in at least fifteen layers of dirt. He clears his voice and starts to sing. The stomps get louder as more people join in, clapping their hands along to the rhythm.

At first, I can't figure out the song but as the chorus begins, I realize it's Stevie Wonder's "Signed, Sealed, Delivered." Lachlan's mouth drops open as the townspeople begin to perform a synchronized dance. Kal's eyes go round as she drops her dad's arm and everyone dances around us.

My dad stares daggers at me as if he knows this is somehow my doing. "Winifred."

I don't bother responding. Not when there's a show going on. And I mean, they're actually really good. Bill's got the voice of a nightingale. Stevie would approve. The beat's perfect, and the singers harmonize so well, and they're even doing some a cappella guitar sounds with their mouths that sound legit.

Old Mrs. Anders performs a pirouette and then leaps into the air like a ballerina. It makes sense she *could* do it since she used to teach ballet about ten years ago, but she retired with a bad knee. Still, she doesn't miss a beat. The group spreads out, drumming hard on the sidewalk with their feet.

Dad flicks me suspicious glances but claps along to the beat. I can probably lie and say this was a flash mob. I mean, if any town in America would do this, it's Honeycrisp Hill. Even though I'm pretty sure I know what caused this. An Enchanted Match.

As the song reaches its final peak, the dancing and

drumming intensify. Bill's voice belts loudly and confidently, and I sort of wish I could have joined in. I know the magic is making them do this, and that I'm responsible for it, yet I can't help but feel that this is *good*. I helped to make the grumpiest, strangest people sing and dance. That can't be witchcraft. And . . .

If I could do *this*, what else am I capable of?

A big smile stretches my cheeks. When have I ever done magic this brilliant?

The performance ends on a high note, and the townspeople shake their heads, a question in their eyes. As if it never happened, they go back to what they were doing before. Preparing their booths, collecting their groceries, strolling down the town square.

"Well . . . that was weird," Kal says.

"What was that?" Lachlan shakes his head, smiling.

"Someone's got some explaining to do," Dad says, frowning at me.

A cackle rips through the wind. A shadow appears, swooping onto the concrete before us, large and imposing. *The* shadow figure, with the long cloak and pointy hat. It's real. It's really here.

The shadow's laughter is full of malice and terror. The townspeople don't notice—maybe they can't see the enchantment? But my dad stiffens beside me. Lachlan's head tilts back. Kal's eyes widen.

"*Winifred.*" My name's a whisper as leaves blow around us in warning. "*I'm coming.*"

When it's over, I have four faces staring at me. My dad, Lachlan, Kal . . . and Esmerelda Diaz, who looks like a cat that caught the mouse.

"*You,*" she says. "I knew it was a Mosley."

"You knew what, exactly?" Dad throws his arm around me and pushes me halfway behind him. Lachlan shifts to stand beside him. Kal, meanwhile, has her mouth dropped open while her ice cream drips down her hand.

Esmerelda's eyes narrow. "There's a wickedness in this town, a wickedness that threatens to break the barriers. And it was her." She points at me. "Step aside. I'm going to take her in—"

"You," Lachlan says calmly, "can't take her anywhere. She's a minor and the way I see it, you haven't showed any evidence that it was Winifred who did it."

Dad shoots him a glance that reads *thank you* before turning back to Esmerelda. "Unless you can prove any of your accusations, we're going home."

Esmerelda huffs. "You have no idea what is happening here. I've calculated, and we have until Halloween. Then the barriers will break, and everything we've been keeping out will come in." She stares down at me. "When that happens, there'll be proof. And I won't just exile her like I did with her no-good mother—I'll take her magic, too."

"My daughter," Dad says, with a scary edge to his voice, "is a powerful enchanter. But even this . . ." He waves his arms around, implying the dancing. "Is beyond the magic of a twelve-year-old. You know as well as I do that kids don't even have access to spells that could do *half* of this. You've got the wrong person and the wrong family."

"We'll see about that," she threatens. Esmerelda turns around and stalks off, her footsteps echoing on the pavement.

My shoulders hunch and I cringe. I cannot lose my magic. I can't be like my mother. I just have to fix it and everything will be okay.

But *how* do I fix it?

And how do I fix it in exactly one week?

Recipe Journal of Winifred Mosley

OOOOH, GIRL-YOU'RE-IN-TROUBLE COOKIES

*A.K.A. "throw in everything you've got
and hope for the best" cookies*

Ingredients:

1 cup butter at room temperature

3/4 cup and 2 tablespoons light brown sugar

1/2 cup sugar

2 eggs

1 teaspoon vanilla

3 cups flour

1 teaspoon baking powder

1 teaspoon baking soda

1/2 teaspoon coarse sea salt

3-3 1/2 cups chocolate chips and chocolate-coated
candies like M&Ms or Reese's Pieces—whatever
you have on hand. The more colorful and
flavorful, the better. **DO NOT STRESS-EAT
THEM or else you won't have enough**

sea salt to sprinkle on top

How to make:

1. Preheat oven to 400°F and set rack in the middle
of oven.

2. Place butter in mixing bowl with both sugars.

3. Beat butter and sugars on medium speed until smooth. This should take about 1-2 minutes until the sugars are completely mixed in.

4. Add the eggs and vanilla, then beat on medium speed just until incorporated with butter and sugars, about 30 seconds.

5. Add the flour, baking powder, baking soda, and salt. Mix until just combined.

6. Pour the chocolate chips into the batter and mix again until just combined. If you succumbed to the stress of life and ate some, it's okay, I forgive you.

7. You can refrigerate the dough for a few hours or overnight or not at all. I didn't notice a difference, but it's good to know you can wait on baking. ☺

8. I used a large cookie scoop, about 3 tablespoons. These spread a bit, not much but they need their space. I put 5-6 cookies per sheet pan; any more than that and they'll spread into a cookie puddle, and it won't be as tasty as that sounds.

9. Sprinkle the tops with sea salt!

10. Bake for 11 minutes or 8-9 minutes for convection

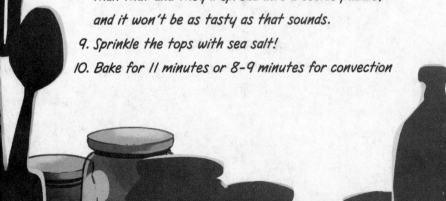

ovens. The cookies are done when the top is a bit golden.

11. Take them out and let them sit on the hot sheet pan till they firm up, about 5 minutes. Move to a cooling rack or plate and make more!

12. Enjoy! And also, if you want to stay out of trouble, these'll help.

16

Kal

During study hall in the school library, Wini and I agree to meet and go over our plans. But when she enters, it seems like our plans are going to be a lot more intense than I would've imagined.

She's wearing a stunning green dress that flares out at her waist and gives her the air of a movie starlet. Her curls are piled high into a loose bun, and her arms are laden with a ton of books. Spellbooks, from the looks of it, including one of my family grimoires. Weirdly, she doesn't look as nervous as I am.

She's barely in her seat when I blurt out the first question. "Are you in trouble?"

After all the singing and dancing and shadow-witch thing, Esmerelda Diaz practically tried to drag her away to magical prison. My dad went over to the bakery with lawbooks last night but he wouldn't let me come.

"Sorta," she huffs. "Wait . . . *Magic to speak, magic to hear, to those who'd harm me make my voice unclear.*"

The moment the words hit my ears, the magic washes over me like a warm breeze. "Where'd you learn that?"

"One of the old Mosley grimoires," she says with a shrug. "Esmerelda Diaz believes I'm the one responsible for calling a wickedness to town."

"That's not even possible. I mean—"

"I might've. In fact, I think I did," she says. I either gasp or choke, either way I can't form words just yet. "See . . . Remember when I said I made a mistake and then I sorta said I did a love spell and it failed?"

"Eh" is all the response I can give.

"Well. That might've, mistakenly—you know, definitely by accident—called a wickedness to town and possibly a shadow thing that keeps whispering my name, and . . . started to break down some barriers or something and could maybe, I don't know, spread the town curse . . . *wider*."

"Wini." I gulp at air like a fish out of water. "You said it was safe."

"It was—it *is* . . ." she replies quickly, as if she still believes it. "Anyway, I know what I gotta do."

"What do we have to do?" I take a book from the pile in front of her. "How do we fix it? If it's just a love spell, can't we just create it ourselves?"

"No, it doesn't work like that. It—"

"You love books, right? So all we have to do is magic." I don't wait for her response. I just dig through the books, looking for counter-spells and anecdotal stories that may have a similar theme to our current situation. When I finally find something that could be useful—a story about a cursed schoolhouse in Massachusetts where all the students could only speak backward for a few weeks—the text says that the townspeople found the solution by banding together and repeating a counter-curse they created. I set the book down. How are we going to do *that*?

I gulp and change the subject quickly. "Well anyway, I realized, you know what we can do? We can do magic to find a love spell. Watch." I sit up straighter and take a deep breath.

"Kal, wait—"

"*Heart and mind, body and soul, shimmer bright what hides in sight.*" I flip the nearest book open and watch as the air around us lights up like fireworks. Reds, greens, and a bit of purple. The book is full of all kinds of colors. Right, now all I have to do is . . . "*Heart and mind, body and soul, purple expand on my command.*"

There's a thunderous *pop*, and I look around to see if a light bulb blew above us. But the sound came from—

Wini's jaw drops. Her eyes grow three sizes, and I can only describe her face as sheer terror. She stands up quickly, knocking some books to the floor. Little pieces of material fall from under her dress and all around her feet. Kids point. Mouths flap open.

Oh. *No.*

Wini bolts to the door, bits of dark purple cotton drifting to the floor in her haste. There's outright laughter now, though I doubt anyone knows why they're laughing. I gnash my teeth together before running over to grab her fallen books.

I think I just exploded her underwear.

17

Wini

Of all things to happen to me, I never expected my underwear to physically explode in front of everyone. They were my lucky pair. The ones I wear when I'm helping make those finnicky, fragile tulip paste wedding cake decorations for Dad or when I'm about to take a Saturday school test.

Or when I'm trying desperately to find a solution for accidentally calling wickedness to town.

Soothing Zimti—a mix of a Danish and a croissant, flattened and filled with buttery cinnamon and brown sugar—is, thankfully, in my backpack as if I packed it just in case something this bizarre would happen. I let out a sigh, my teeth sinking into the deliciously warm pastry. But after three massive bites, I still don't feel soothed, calm, or even remotely composed. I only feel uncomfortable.

Of all the days to wear my emerald-green shift dress, why today? I'm sitting on top of the toilet lid, my backpack by my feet, my underwear completely gone. I should have taught Kal how that spell works, but I just . . . I wipe my sugary fingers on a piece of toilet paper when a shadow appears beneath my door.

"Winifred . . ."

The sound of wind picks up, whispering something I can't quite hear. My breath catches in my throat.

"Hello?" my voice calls out timidly. "Who's there?"

The sounds intensify as if I'm in the center of a storm. The bathroom door swings open and the shadow disappears. I gulp at the air, my lungs expanding too fast from holding my breath.

"I had to search every bathroom for you," Kal says through the stall door. "So . . . about that . . ."

"Do not talk to me about *that*, Kaliope Clarke. Not a single word." I put enough edge into my voice to keep from stammering. I'm in full crisis mode now. Yes, the way people stared at me, laughed and pointed, hurt. Yes, it'll haunt me. But I'm already being haunted or hunted by something I don't fully understand, which is way worse. "I'm going to sneak out of study hall, I have to go somewhere."

She's quiet for a few seconds. "Where are you going?"

"Home for new undies, and then I'm going to see someone about undoing that spell. I was going to research it myself but . . ." But there are no books that'll have a solution for an experimental spell. Besides, I'd planned on seeing Old Miss Maple anyway to ask her more about

Coraline, just not so early. And I'm in enough trouble already, skipping the rest of school will barely matter.

Esmerelda Diaz is convinced I'm responsible for the dance number yesterday (which I am), believes I've performed wicked magic (which I may have?), somehow summoned a wickedness (which, *what*? But yeah, likely), and though she can't prove any of it, she said she will. Annnnd the town could be destroyed. So it's not going well.

The only thing I can try is to undo the spell before it gets me stripped of my magic and exiled or thrown in jail. They don't throw twelve-year-olds in jail, right? I had good intentions, after all. The entire reason I did the spell was for the bakery. But it was all for nothing.

The bell rings and there's a flurry of activity outside the halls that's a parade of both feet and loud voices drifting in. Kal tries to talk but she's drowned out by the cacophony. The door opens and closes and I imagine she left to get to class. It's just as well. I'm used to being alone.

As the sound dies down, I pack away the rest of the Zimti and rise. Pushing the stall door open, I'm surprised to see Kal leaning against the sink, scrolling through her phone.

I rinse my hands and dry them with a paper towel. "What are you still doing here?"

Her head rises and she puts her hands on her hips. "I'm coming with you. I have many skills including but not limited to impersonations, last-minute disguises, jokes that diffuse situations quickly, um . . . I read a lot of books and that sometimes comes in handy? Also, three out of five people have called me charming. So—"

"You made that last one up." I shake my head. "You shouldn't get involved with this. And anyway, Old Miss Maple is not the type you want to meet. One"—I count on my fingers—"she always requests I help her pick apples on her orchard. Two, she is the grouchiest woman and is quite possibly three hundred years old, and, if you ask her about it, she'll turn you into a teapot and fill you with hot water, which also really hurts. Don't ask me how many times I made that mistake. And three, she doesn't like most people." I swing my backpack onto my back.

"Stop pushing me away, Wini. I'm not scared of Old Miss Maple. I'm as much a part of this . . . magical town as you are. And I want to know it like you do. And also, I'm your friend, so stop being all you and be more . . . me."

It's not eloquent, but I stop. We stare at each other. "I can only be sunshine and lollipops once in a while. Not like you."

She sets her jaw. "I'm not sunshine or lollipops. When I'm feeling good, I'm happy and bubbly and maybe even funny. I'm ridiculous. When I'm anxious, I'm . . . none of those things. But I try. I put on a good face, and I fake it till I feel it."

I purse my lips. "What if you keep faking it and you end up not feeling it?"

At first, she's quiet, and I worry that I've pushed too far. Like I always do.

"I *will* feel it." Her tone is strong, resolute. "Sometimes, it feels like . . . it's like floating in the ocean. Sometimes you tread water and you get so tired you think you might give up, and sometimes you pull things, people, toward you that can help you float. It's a cycle. I'll stay afloat. I have medicine, a therapist, family, and I have you."

Suddenly, there's a lump in my throat. I try to swallow it down.

She steps closer. "And *you* have *me*."

I've never had anyone really . . . try before. It feels good. "I'm happy to be your buoy."

"Oh shut up, Wini." She laughs. "Let's go see this enchanter."

A major drawback of small-town life: Skipping school is never worth it if one of the obnoxious townspeople catches you. They'll rat me out in minutes, and the last thing I need is Aunt Maddie punishing me. Having Kal with me won't help either, since people are bound to notice the new girl. But it's too late now and besides, I still need new underwear.

Getting out of the building is easy enough, but then it becomes a minefield. We live on Main Street, out in the open. Which means I've got to sneak in through the courtyard.

Which means I've got to go through the woods.

I don't know why I'm afraid of the woods near the town line of Brookston. They're not at all dark and mysterious. I mean, yeah, I saw a pack of wolves there once when I was a kid sledding down a hill, but they mostly just watched me and whimpered a few times. I figured they were hungry so I tossed a few snacks to them. But there's something about the woods that worries me.

"Do you know you've been humming some weird song the entire time we've been walking through the field?" Kal says, lips quirking.

"It's my sneaking song. Isn't it helping you feel calm about not getting caught?"

She steps over a fallen branch. "I don't really care about it. After the whole underwear incident, I can say I was consoling you."

I snort. "Like anyone would care that I need consoling." We cross through the final bit of the track and into the woods. I keep my irrational fears to myself.

"Why not?"

My answer doesn't take long. "Because half the town hates me since my mom did . . . you know, all those things."

"Unlike me," she responds, and I toss her the side-eye. "I can't imagine how it would feel to be born into a place where they hate you because of something your mom did."

"Yeah, well . . ." is all I can really say. I remember being six and getting a brand-new bicycle. I rode up and down the street showing everyone and waving and laughing. I felt so free to get around on my own. I even thought I could deliver pastries in a red cape like Little Red Riding Hood. But the glares I got were so intense, I stopped riding. I stopped smiling. The bakery is the only place that feels like home. And though I'm happy to have Kal now, there's still a lot of painful history in this town that won't go away just because I've got a new friend.

The tree roots creak and the leaves scatter in the breeze.

"This place gives me the creeps," Kal says, her fingers grazing an old oak that skims the sky.

"Me too," I admit.

Something howls, far off but not as far off as I'd like.

"What was that?" Kal's voice goes up three octaves. "Did you hear that?"

"Wolves." I grimace, rubbing my arms for much-needed warmth. The temperature has dropped at least ten degrees since we entered these woods. I've never experienced anything like it, and I've been in these woods my entire life. "Just wolves."

"You have wolves out here? For real?" Kal stops dead in her tracks. "Next you're going to tell me you have bears, too."

I smile at her while waving her forward. No time to stop, something has me on edge, my skin prickling. "Bears *and* coyotes."

"Oh no," she says, scampering toward me. "That's like an eighty-three percent chance of an attack."

I shake my head. "That's not a real statistic."

"You're not a hundred percent incorrect." She winks and I roll my eyes.

"Double negative," I mutter. Oddly her words comfort me, even as my fear escalates the deeper into the woods we go. "Why are you always so goofy?"

She grins. "Seventy-eight percent of my friends ask me that."

I chuckle, despite the uneasiness coiling in the pit of my stomach. "There's something different about the woods. At night, from my bedroom window, I hear things. I see things, too . . ." My mind travels to the shadow witch in her long cloak. To the darkness outside

Saturday school and my bathroom door. But no, now's not the time to speak about that. It would make it real, even more frightening. "I've been seeing weird things."

Kal picks up the pace, maneuvering through the dense trees behind me. "Have you told anyone?"

"Nah." I thought about it but what can anyone do, really? Dad would be like, *Wini, there's nothing here.* He'd think I made it up. He's already explained away the shadow witch in the sky after the flash-mob dance.

There's a scuttle somewhere in the distance, maybe a squirrel, but it doesn't sound like one. It sounds bigger. A twig snaps beneath my heavy boot, and the air seems to change.

"I can feel you, enchanters . . ."

The words float through the trees toward us and swirl around like cocoa powder sifted atop a hot chocolate. Whatever it is, it's not human.

Kal nearly leaps out of her skin and reaches out to take my hand. I let her thread our fingers together. "Who's that? Who's there? What do you want?"

There's a giggle on the wind. "Oh, you're *baby* enchanters."

We're about to bolt when a shiny figure appears between the trees. A girl. She smiles at us. Her silver eyes shine bright and her skin is gray like translucent paper. Silver hair whips in the wind. For a moment, the girl in front of us has as much color and depth as a black-and-white picture.

I let out a startled gasp, and Kal squeezes my hand. The girl holds a paper-thin finger to her lips, shushing us. My breath catches in my throat and my heart races.

She's not an enchanter. Not *normal*. You'd think that my understanding of the magical world around town would make me less surprised, but whatever she is, I haven't seen her type before. And that's a scary, scary thing.

Terror sends goose bumps up my arms. A ghost. A creature that's not supposed to be here.

"You're both so young," the unhuman girl tells us.

My fingers search for purchase against a tree as I stare at her uneasily. Her silver eyes round. My words stammer out. "W-we're old enough."

The apparition smiles, glowing like pearly white fondant on a wedding cake despite it being daytime. "Do your parents know you're here?"

"I . . . I . . ." Kal's legs shake beside me, and I hold her hand tight.

The girl giggles again, and it's warm even though she emits a frigid breeze. "You don't know, do you? The spell you cast . . ." She smiles. "The barriers of the town are crumbling. Powerful magic is falling apart, curses are breaking." She tosses her head to the side, shimmering like moonlight. "I've only just arrived in Honeycrisp Hill, thanks to you. Everything's changing." She perks up—if a ghost can do anything perkily. "Exciting, isn't it?"

A million questions run across my mind, but the moment I open my mouth, only one falls out. "The spell? My spell?"

"It's letting all of us in. All kinds of creatures—ones that have died, ones that live forever, some that howl at the moon, and sparkle under starry, starry nights, and trick humans for a bit of fun. Oh"—she laughs—"everything is about to be very different for you, little enchanters."

She turns her head suddenly, the smile dropping from her translucent face. She flinches as if she can feel the cold. "Gotta go now, and you should, too." She winks and then she's gone. Into thin air. As if she was never really here.

"What . . . what was that?" Kal asks, staring at the space where the girl used to be.

"A ghost," I say softly. I yank her over another thicket, collecting my thoughts, when the trees croak and the ground shakes. There are footsteps, heavy, terrible footsteps, that grow louder and closer. Mist pours softly through the trees, obscuring everything around us. The wind whistles and the cold seeps deeper through my jacket. Goose bumps travel up my bare legs. My breath is short.

"Who . . . who's there now?" Kal's voice cracks, and I try to steady her.

Only the silence greets us, and an unnerving sense of apprehension.

"Kal, it's okay. Everything's okay." The lie doesn't sound convincing even to my ears. I grip her a little tighter while pushing her away from the sound. But there's nowhere to go in the light.

A whisper moves gently through the air. *"Little enchanters in the woods dark and deep. I wonder if your blood will taste so sweet . . ."*

Okay, never mind. This isn't okay, we have to go, even if we can't see. I pull Kal's hand hard. *"Run."*

With her hand in mine, I pull her at breakneck speed through the trees, only guessing our direction. A few feet away, there's a patch of light and we make for it when Kal stumbles over a tree branch. I try to grab her, but her ankle is stuck underneath. She looks up at me, her face contorted in horror.

"Where are you going, children? Don't you know you've crossed into my domain? It's only fair . . ."

The whisper is everywhere and nowhere at once. Kal gasps for air.

The brambles seem to tighten around us. Sounds grow louder. My breath mixes with the sudden fog as footsteps thud heavier, closer. Kal's still trying to pull herself free and no matter how hard I tug, she's stuck. Little whimpers leave her mouth. I jump between her and whatever remains unseen. It's closing in on us.

A sentence loops through my mind. My voice shakes. *"Heart and mind, body and soul, shimmer bright what hides in sight!"*

Normally the spell works. It's the easiest, safest spell. Until now. There are no colors, no emotions. Just darkness that wisps around us like plumes of smoke, threatening to steal the very breath from our lungs.

Kal lets out an egg-curdling scream.

My eyes are glued to the growing mass in front of us. My feet seem to sink farther into the earth, not letting me go. I want to run. I want to hide. The darkness blots out the sun, blots out our hope. Blots out any solution I may have.

"Wini," Kal begs. "Run. You have to leave me."

"I won't . . ." I trail off as the darkness approaches, barely a foot away now. My entire body quakes. "I'm not leaving you."

"Little enchanters," it hisses, *"in the dark, treacherous wood. Who shall protect you now that your guardians are gone and the barriers break?"*

"Go," Kal whispers.

I put my hand on my hips. I will not be cowed. Not today and not any other day. Fear may try to overtake me, but I'm Winifred Theodora Mosley. And I don't back down. "No way."

I wish the darkness had a face I could punch. Maddie told me Mosleys aren't cowards. We don't run from problems. We stand tall.

It encircles us, leaving only a sliver of light.

"*Heart and mind, body and soul . . .*" Rhyme, I need a rhyme . . .

Kal stares up at me, panic painting her pretty face, but she finally finds her voice. "I cast you out, evil . . ." And then she glances at me, her teeth clenched.

"Seriously, Kal, what rhymes with evil?"

The darkness slithers closer, nearly touching my toes.

Her eyes brighten. "Weevil? Upheaval?"

I begin again. "*Heart and mind, body and soul—*"

Kal's voice rises, sharp and crisp. "*I cast you out, evil, where you can cause no more upheaval!*"

The dark wind stops moving, and for a second I think we've won. But then it laughs, a hideous and cringey thing that causes me to stumble back. It keeps laughing as if we told the funniest joke it's ever heard. Maybe we did.

I'm about to try again when the whites of Kal's eyes blacken at the edges. Vines writhe from around her feet and arc toward the ominous mass before us. Her words, crisp and deep, send shivers down my spine and goose bumps up my arms.

"*Ticktock, goes the clock. One to minute, one to hour, stop them both with my power.*"

The world stands still. Neither of us moves. The blackness in Kal's eyes matches the darkness threatening us. And yet, her spell is cast, a spell different than any I've ever seen, heard, or performed. Her words ring in my ears. The darkness listens to her, and just . . . stops. The spirals halt in midair.

We have no time to appreciate it, no idea how long it'll last. I rip Kal's foot from under the tree and pull her to standing.

"*Winifred . . . I'm coming,*" the wind whispers somewhere above us. The shadow witch is near and honestly, I cannot handle any more of this spooky place. With Kal's arm through mine, we run, not stopping once to look back.

18

Kal

My heart hammers in my chest and my lungs feel as if they can't get full. We reach Wini's backyard, and then keep going till we get to the courtyard. We collapse on the stones leading from the grass to the back door.

We almost, possibly, *died*. I need answers. I need to understand. Something happened to me, to us, back there and we have to know why. Violet's spell . . . it worked, but it felt different. Almost wrong.

"Don't ask me what that was," Wini says, as if she can read my mind. "I don't know. And if it wasn't for your spell, I'm not sure we would have made it out of those woods. Where did you learn that?"

"It doesn't matter. At least it helped." I can't tell her about Violet, she wouldn't understand. Which means I'm keeping secrets from my one and only real friend outside of a book. "We need to know what that was."

"Agreed." Wini pushes herself to stand and extends her hand to me. "Maybe we can ask Miss Maple. But . . . we're not supposed to go through those woods. They're off-limits. We can't tell anyone we were there."

"If my dad knows how close we just got to instant death, he'd flip. You're right."

"I know I'm right. I'm usually right." She purses her lips.

I take her hand. "You're right like seventy-five percent of the time."

She tosses me a grin. The moment of levity almost gets my heart rate to stabilize. Almost. Her grin slips. "What happened to *you* back there?"

Good question. One minute I was there, staring up at the darkness, the next, we were running. "I don't know. I just did the spell."

"I think . . . I'm worried that your magic's not what it's supposed to be. There's something different about it."

I stare at her. "What do you mean? You think because I'm not a word enchanter, I'm . . . a witch?" The thought of Violet flashes in my mind.

"No," Wini says quickly. "I think your magic is still figuring itself out. But we should keep an eye on it. What I saw back there, it wasn't . . ." She trails off. "It's not important right now. I don't know anything more than you."

"Are you scared? What did you see?"

"I don't know what I saw." She shakes her head. "Do you want to come up or stay down here?"

"I'll stay. Go get your underwear." I try to pretend that

entire thing didn't just happen. That I'm fine. Totally fine.

She nods and slides inside the back door quietly enough I think she's had practice.

What if the Agency's here for *me*? What if my magic's wrong somehow? What if—

"Okay, let's go." Wini comes down wearing high-waisted jeans, a white blouse tucked in, her green trench open, and—I kid you not—high-top Converse with an apple pattern on them. Her hair's back in a big, curly ponytail with an ocher bandanna. Instead of her bright red frames, she's got on tortoiseshell ones. I'm convinced not a single other person in the universe can pull off this look but her.

"How did you get dressed so fast?" I stare at her, mouth agog.

She shrugs. "Magic. Right," she says, head held high. "To the orchard."

"Mm-hmm," I respond, falling in step behind her. We creep along the backs of stores until we're at the end of Main Street, in a little triangular park with a playground, fountain, and splash pad for kids that probably got a lot of use in the summer. The air's a lot less nippy than in the woods, and I'm grateful for it. "So are we going to continue talking about that thing that happened back there?"

Wini juts her chin out, tilting her head to the side. "It was . . . I didn't know what to do. I don't like feeling like that. They don't teach us to defend ourselves."

There's frustration in her voice. Suddenly, she's not the Winifred Mosley who stared down living darkness, but a girl who doesn't have everything figured out. She stops, her eyes peering into mine. She slumps. Tired but not defeated.

"I won't let that happen again. I won't be caught unprepared like that again." And the Wini I know is back. Silence spans the space between us as the wind rustles the leaves and the teeter-totters squeal, hitting the dirt. Wini takes a deep breath, standing taller, more resolute.

"All right, let's go, then." I grab her arm and shove it through mine like she did before. "You and me are going to save everything."

The corner of her lip lifts. "You're so optimistic."

"Better than your everything-is-doomed approach."

We walk up the sidewalk to a hilly road ahead. She's quiet for a few beats as we climb, passing by beautiful, quaint homes with wraparound porches, patches of manicured bushes, and a million Halloween decorations.

Down the block, Esmerelda Diaz stands all in black, unmoving, staring at us.

"You see her, right?" I ask.

"Yeah . . ." Wini says softly, an edge of fear in her voice. "I swear I've even seen her in my dreams. That's why we need to rush." Wini pulls me through dense bushes that stand before a tall wooden fence.

"How do we—?"

She smirks. "Enchantment."

Wini steps through, tugging me along with her. We walk through the fence that looked so real and wooden and strong but was nothing more than illusion. A sound escapes my mouth. This world is amazing.

Our feet step onto intensely bright green grass. Trees stick out of the ground, their branches heavy with sparkling red apples. There are too many to count, too many to see where the orchard begins and ends. The sky even looks bluer here. It's unreal. Gorgeous. The air smells sweet and spicy.

"Don't touch the apples," Wini whispers. "If you touch without permission, she'll get angry."

"How would she know?" I whisper back. The grass is soft beneath my boots. I find myself wanting to lie down on it and take a nap.

"She knows everything. Old Miss Maple already knows we're here." She tilts her head to the side, standing straight.

Before my eyes, a pink glittery bubble materializes out

of thin air like that old movie Dad loves, *The Wizard of Oz*. I half expect the person inside to be wearing a ball gown and a sparkly crown.

The queen that bursts out from the bubble smiles. "Hiya there, dolls." She's got dark brown skin, wears sequined overalls, a tie-dyed yellow sweater, and her bouffant of hair is a shade of midnight blue, complete with pearls that twinkle like stars. Her makeup is impeccable, her lashes extraordinarily long. And on her feet are the rubiest of red slippers.

When she catches me staring at them, her grin widens. "Too much?"

I laugh. "Not at all." She's just not what I expected. "You're Old Miss Maple?"

The smile melts into a deep scowl. "Who you calling old?"

I cringe. "I'm—"

She cuts me off with a loud, vivacious laugh that shakes an apple right off the tree next to us. She catches it in one hand. "I'm just kidding. I'm Loretta. Old Miss Maple, Ada's her name, is my partner. She's in a real mood today, sugar." This she says to Wini before taking a big bite.

Wini doesn't miss a beat. "It's really important, promise."

Loretta eyes Wini's attire and bunches her lips together

in approval. "In that outfit, honey, it must be. One day I'm gonna learn your fashion secrets." She glances my way and is decidedly less than impressed.

I like to think my rebel-girl-meets-artist look makes me blend in well while adding a bit of personality. But around these two, I feel underdressed.

Loretta surprises me with a wink. "I like your devil-may-care thing going on. Kaliope, right?"

"How did you know?" I squeak, the compliment heating my cheeks.

Loretta hitches a brow. "Everyone talks in Honeycrisp Hill. I even know about your grandpa, Ian. Surprised they let him leave the Agency. Ya know they don't mess around, and once they have an agent who's good at what they do, they make it impossible to leave. Lots of wickedness out there in this big magical world, and the Enchantment Agency plays an important role in eradicating it . . . sometimes."

"What did he do?" I ask.

"I think that's his story to tell when he's ready. Can you imagine searching out and arresting dangerous creatures for twenty years? The things he must've seen . . ." Loretta nods her head in the direction of the house. "Before I take you there, you know the deal. Pick enough apples for two pies, and do be careful, dears, the poisonous ones look especially tempting this year." The edges of her slippers touch a large woven basket that has appeared out of nowhere.

Wini smiles. "You got it."

Before Loretta walks off, I have to ask. "It's late October and your orchard is full. It's nearly off-season . . . how? And what do you mean by *poisonous*?"

Loretta chuckles. "You really are new, huh? Well, this is the biggest producer of enchanted apples this side of the globe. Why do you think they call it Honeycrisp Hill? That's our number one apple." She shrugs. "You'd think New York would be number one since they got loads of orchards, but their temps are a little too warm. We ship ours worldwide, all year long. Even the grass is magical. Can't you feel it?"

I nod. "It's soft and I feel like I want to nap on it."

"Mm-hmm. But don't do it." She winks again.

My eyes bulge. "Is it poisonous, too?"

"It's just Ada wouldn't like you sleeping on her grass." Loretta talks a mile a minute, and I find myself wanting to ask her a million more questions. "And enchanted apple trees sometimes produce poisonous apples."

I have no idea what to say to that.

Loretta flashes me another smile before whispering a spell and disappearing inside another brilliant pink bubble.

Wini shifts beside me. "Right, the apples. We need

twenty of them and the only way to get them down is to make them laugh."

My mouth flaps open. "And how do we do that?"

Wini grimaces like I've just said the silliest thing. "We tell them jokes, obviously."

I think my eyebrows melt into my hairline. "We have to tell the trees jokes . . . to get apples?"

She nods, drifting over to a tree. "Okay, so. Why does Peter Pan always fly?" She's silent, waiting for the comedic beat. "Because he neverlands!"

An apple somewhat hesitantly falls from the tree.

"Dang." Wini tosses me a look. "That joke landed me two last time."

I crinkle my nose and walk over to another tree. "What did the pirate say on his eightieth birthday?" I put on a funny accent. "Aye, matey." Two apples fall, and I bolt to catch them. I grin at Wini. "Looks like I'm better than you."

She smiles and all the tension and worry and scariness from earlier seems to melt away for the moment. "Oh, it's on!"

Wini and I saunter over to two different trees. "What did the inspector find after an explosion at the French cheese factory?" she says. "De Brie!" That lands her another solo apple. "Tough crowd today."

I wiggle a little, getting into position to catch two

more apples. "Why did the Romanian stop reading?" I wag my eyebrows. "To give his Bucharest." Wini rolls her eyes but I get two apples. "You're going to have to do better to beat me."

She narrows her gaze, stepping over to another tree. "What do you call a fake noodle?" She raises her brows. "An impasta!" This time she does get two, and she smirks my way like an insufferable know-it-all.

I switch it up. "Wini's underwear exploded at school today; she must have been too excited to study!" I laugh at my own joke, remembering her absolute mortification. Three apples fall. "The best underwear jokes are brief." Another apple falls.

I've found the best source of jokes now. I really could be a comedian.

"Who makes the best exploding underwear?" I stifle a giggle watching Wini's face turn rosy. "Fruit of the Boom!" Two more apples land gently on the grass. My collection is bigger, and better yet, I'm beating Wini at something. She's all flustered but clutching her side as if she might laugh herself.

"Here's a short poem. Roses are red, violets are blue. Wini's underwear is purple, and everyone saw them, too!" More apples. "I am so good at this. I think I've found my calling in life."

Wini's head falls back on her shoulders, and she

lets out a small laugh. "You're the worst, you know that."

"One more joke and we'll have enough. Wanna do the honors?"

She rolls her eyes one more time. "Why does a pirate wear underwear? To hide his booty!"

Apples rain down all over the place.

19

Wini

raveling by bubble with nearly two dozen apples and
Kal, who is guffawing the entire time, is less than fun.
The air is terribly sweet but cold.

"How big is this place? I feel like we've been traveling
for half an hour."

I sigh, staring down at the thousands of trees below us.
"Bubble riding takes forever. It's only been a few minutes. But while we wait, I need to tell you something."

"Me too. You first." She presses her head against the
translucent pink film separating us from the sky and an
extremely long and painful drop.

"Ada Maple looks as old as my Aunt Maddie, but
don't be fooled. Ada and Loretta are hundreds of years
old. Secondly, Ada will likely only agree to a set number
of questions, and I will need every single one of them, so
don't ask anything, okay?"

She nods. "You got it."

"Lastly, we're going to make apple pie. Every time I
come here, there's an unofficial rule that they'll want
me to make my family recipe for them." This time I

smile. I'm more than a little proud of our pies. I grew up making them and improved the recipe for the crust last year.

"Okay, so I help you make apple pie, anything else?"

"Yes. Don't say anything at all offensive, especially about her cat, Mr. Jay Catsby. He's a jerk. Knocking over stuff all the time and trying to climb on your head. And whatever you do—"

The bubble begins the descent, and I lose track of my thoughts.

"Whatever you do?" Kal asks, eyes wide.

"Oh, right." My mind's all over the place trying to decide the questions I want to ask. Sometimes Ada's a genie-in-a-lamp type of literal—when she's in a mood, she will find any way out of answering questions she doesn't want to. It's very frustrating. It's why I only come here when I really need help. "Whatever you do, do not, under any circumstances, offer to do her a favor. Promise me."

Kal throws her hands up. "Please, like anyone would ask me for a favor." I cock an eyebrow. "I promise."

"Good."

We plummet calmly from the sky toward an oversize red barn. In the back, workers roll barrels of glimmering apples toward a massive press machine. The apple cider it'll make is used in our apple cider doughnuts and our Christmas ham dinner. It's my second favorite fall-slash-winter drink. (Everything's secondary to hot chocolate.)

Loretta and Ada stand against the barn door. Where Loretta is all sparkles and larger than life, Ada is small and intimidating. She looks like an artist: She's in all black, her curly black hair's pulled into a tight bun high on her head, a purple pencil stuck in it sideways. Her cat-eye glasses remind me of one of those librarians from an old movie. Sharp and pointy, all-seeing. She's terrifying for someone so tiny.

"That's her?"

"Yup," I say as we touch down. Kal runs her hands over her plain white tee. "Nervous?"

The bubble begins to dissipate into smaller pink bubbles that look like the ones that come out of those little wands kids have at every town festival.

"Completely," she says softly.

I nudge her with my shoulder. "I got you." I lift the basket with one hand and swing my other arm through hers.

She grins at me as we step on the grass toward Loretta and Ada.

"Why'd you bring the new one?" Ada asks, her voice gravelly. She has a deep voice that would be perfectly suited for a jazz band.

"She's my friend." I smile at Kal, and Loretta sighs happily before clapping her hands.

"Finally."

Ada's gaze narrows. "You've known her, what, two weeks?" It's not at all surprising she and Aunt Maddie are friends. They are the most unfun people around. Always suspicious, ready to rain on a parade . . . usually mine.

"Sometimes people just click," Kal answers, her voice a bit stronger as she takes a tentative step forward. "We brought your apples."

"Good." She eyes me. "You get three questions. Three."

I want to say that last time she gave me five, that I've never been in such a dangerous and bizarre predicament. That I need *help*. But I only nod. I know better than to argue.

"You'll make me two of my favorite apple pies. And in return I won't tell Esmerelda Diaz about anything you say here or that this one's . . . different." Ada points at Kal. "Lucky for you, the Enchantment Agency holds no sway in this orchard."

"Not even an ounce." Loretta laughs. "Bet they wish they could get their hands on our Ada, but after that incident—"

"Loretta." Ada's voice is low. "As I was saying, I can see how someone's magic forms inside of them. Wolves, vampires, witches, ghosts, goblins, malevolent things that go bump in the night. Winifred's magic is the strongest presence in town. I can see her miles away, so shiny and bright. But yours, little girl, is just as powerful, and where Wini's is one big, focused energy, yours is all over the place. You can ask me about it, but it'll be taken out of the three questions. And something tells me Winifred has a lot to ask, right?"

Kal's eyes widen, mouth hanging open. I elbow her and whisper, "Later, okay?" Finding out what that thing in the woods was, the ghost girl, and figuring out if I accidentally summoned a shadow witch—these things are urgent. More urgent than Kal's magic, at least right now.

"Deal," I say. "Two apple pies. Three questions."

We step over the threshold into the barn house, the magic inside coating our skin like a fine mist from a waterfall, and just as cool. It leaves little drops of dew on our hands. I've asked about it, but each time Ada just tells me it's for my own good.

Kal's gaze roves through the mudroom, where coats of all shapes and sizes hang from the walls. I nudge her foot with mine, alerting her that we have to take our shoes off. She huffs, bending over to untie her combat boot laces. I kick my Converse off.

Loretta slides her shoes onto the rickety rack beside a

pair of golden rain boots. "The sudden rain has created the worst mud."

I shrug. It's New England and fall; it's never predictable, even before it started being affected by my spell.

The scent of lemongrass mingling with lavender permeates the air and soothes my senses, making me decidedly calmer. Ada and Loretta make sure people feel like they can let their guards down here, which is both nice and dangerous.

Kal and I follow them down the black-and-white halls. Old photos hang on the walls. Loretta and Ada through the years. Timeless. Their faces never change, but their surroundings do. The barn gets bigger, their outfits look older. As we pass the last one, Ada stands beside a wooden wagon while Loretta sits on it, covered in hay. She's smiling, her eyes crinkling at the edges.

We enter their vibrant kitchen. It reminds me of something Julia Child would've worked in. Two islands, various stovetops, copper pans melded to the walls (probably when they found out those pans are better decoration than cookware), antique signs for milk (which used to cost five cents a gallon, apparently), an oversize dining table that's painted like a rainbow, and open cabinets that present a million mismatched plates and utensils. I set the basket of apples on the nearest island.

"Double, double, apples and tools! Oven on, follow the

rules. *Enchanters work, without mistake, two pies they must make,*" Ada casts. Then she winks at me. "Now bake."

I smile as the tools fly from their spots and land gently on the tables before us. Ada loves to do this. *Show-off*. It impresses Kal, though, who watches in awe as the apples tumble from the basket and begin peeling themselves. That's the easy part. The rest is up to me.

Loretta turns the radio on, and I inwardly sigh as Stevie Wonder's voice croons into the kitchen. "Higher Ground" plays and Loretta starts dancing around, trying to get Ada to join in. She says no, but soon she will. No one can resist dancing with Loretta. She brings out the joy in everyone.

"Kal, can you put four cups of flour in that bowl?" She nods while I grab the brown sugar, cinnamon, and salt, adding the right amount to the growing pile of flour. I snatch a pound of sweet cream butter from the refrigerator and begin cutting it up into small pats.

With the edge of the knife, I add it to the bowl, then demonstrate for Kal how to mix everything until it's crumbly. Our fingers mingle together, working the flour and butter slowly, never using our thumbs so as not to heat it up too much.

It's then I decide to ask the first question, choosing my words very carefully. "A few days ago, I swear the sky darkened, and something called my name. Today, we saw a ghost in the woods on the other side of town and there was a dark presence that called us enchanters and I think it was going to hurt us. What's happening?"

Ada moves her shoulders back and forth next to Loretta. "Outside Honeycrisp Hill, there are creatures that try to come in or lure you out. They've gotten bolder recently, but they've always been here. They're attracted to magic. They *feed* on magic." Ada pauses, taking a deep breath. "Townspeople used to take their true forms, so they could defend the town. We could expand our borders. Your mother, well . . ." Ada plucks an apple from the table and takes a bite. My fingertips continue to work the butter and flour together, and I have to remind myself to be gentle as I wait. "Unfortunately, after your mother's spell, the townspeople were . . . unable to change, unable to protect us. And the wickedness outside only grows."

Kal opens her mouth, and I shake my head. "I know you have a lot to ask but I need these three questions."

"But—"

I shake my head. I know it's not fair. Ada is the oldest enchanter in Honeycrisp Hill, maybe even the oldest in the world. Loretta's not far behind. Because of this, Ada doesn't like to share too much about the past with us or anyone—she says it "sullies the present." And that "enchantment wasn't always so safe." Aunt Maddie especially doesn't like me poking around in the past, not when the Mosley past includes Coraline. She'd be mad if she knew I was here, even more than if she knew I skipped school. She'd put me on dish duty for a month.

Once the flour is done, Kal and I rinse our hands. I wipe them on the kitchen towel hanging on the oven handle and then take a tray of ice from the freezer. Kal fills a bowl with water at my direction, and I plonk several ice cubes inside, letting it chill.

Meanwhile, we use the apple slicer to core and cut the apples. I douse them in cinnamon, sugar, a dash of cardamom, and an even bigger dash of nutmeg, and Kal tosses in flour. She mixes that together as I attend the ice water. Using a tablespoon, I add spoon after spoon until a dough forms with a fork. I dump it out on the table and gently knead it into a ball. Kal opens the freezer and I toss it inside to chill before we wash our hands again.

Second question.

"I did a spell Grandma wrote called An Enchanted Match." Loretta sighs hopelessly again but I have to continue, even though my mouth suddenly feels dry. "I thought if I could tweak and test the spell, use my dad as the subject, it would absorb into my bread, bring him love, and give us Love without needing to source it. I would save the bakery . . ." I trail off and lean against the counter, collecting myself. "That's why Stevie Wonder's been playing around town. Why people have been breaking out into song and dance. Why my dad"—I look at Kal—"might be into your dad. But now I know I unintentionally did witchcraft and summoned a wickedness."

I share a glance with Kal that infers we'll talk about it later. I want us to be honest with each other.

"Esmerelda Diaz is threatening to do . . . something to me, but she can't prove I've done anything wrong yet. What do I do?"

Loretta throws her hand over her mouth and Ada takes a seat at the table. She glances out the window and then turns back to me.

"Bernice told me about An Enchanted Match. I read the spell. The magic it requires is bigger than most could perform because it works in ways you can't predict. I'd say I'm surprised you had the magic to do it, but then you are powerful, and you are Coraline's daughter." Ada exhales slowly. "It's like a game of chess. To get the king, you need to move the queen. An Enchanted Match moves the pieces around in mysterious ways. And the love it's seeking, the soulmate aspect of it, isn't always romantic. It can be friends." She eyes

Kal and me. "It can be family. It all comes together some-how. But your problem isn't that you did wicked magic by casting this spell. Your problem is that this spell opens a door to the world beyond Honeycrisp Hill. It breaks down the town's barriers and existing spells to complete itself." She stops for a minute, her eyes a bit wild. "You didn't summon a wickedness, Winifred. You let the wickedness in because it's part of the enchanted match. You just don't know which part yet. No one will until it has fulfilled its role. The spell won't end until all the pieces have moved toward their rightful destination."

"Halloween," I mutter as her words hit me. What have I done? I remember reading Grandma Bernice's warning: *Could possibly dissolve preexisting spells to finalize and sta-bilize itself.* I hadn't really considered what that meant.

Loretta crosses the room and pulls me into a hug. "I know how much the bakery means to you."

I hug her back tightly, my eyes getting a bit misty until Ada interrupts, her gaze on me.

Ada regards me slowly. "What do you want to do, Winifred?"

I huff. "End the spell so I don't get in trouble and lose my magic."

"I see." Ada sniffs. "We still don't understand what Coraline did, but breaking the barriers . . . if the curse is still in effect, it *might* spread. Or it might free everyone. It may not be your fault but Esmerelda will blame you," she adds. "This shadow that's coming, she could be wicked. She could be anything. She could be the missing accomplice they searched for all those years ago. Either way, Esmerelda will strip you of your magic, send you away. It's a tough decision for sure." She pauses, taking a sip of her tea. "I can see why you'd want to break the spell before it can change everything, for better or worse. It is easier to desire the known than the unknown."

I nod. I know what my third question has to be, but I don't want to ask it yet.

With the chilled dough on the wooden bench, I reach for rolling pins and a pizza cutter. Together, we roll out four massive circles, just thick enough to form two delicious crusts, and cut two of them into strips. Kal covers the pie dishes the way I tell her and adds half the apples to each. We lattice the top, under and over until they're perfect, brush them with egg wash, and sprinkle on a little cinnamon sugar. A few strips remain, so I flatten them before shaping them into apples with leafy tendrils. I rub them in cinnamon to make them just a bit darker, and stick them to the top of the pie. And then we slide them into the hot, waiting oven.

I stand up, my back against the cabinets. "How do I break the spell?"

Ada stares at nothing in particular, mumbling nonsense, as she is wont to do sometimes when presented with a difficult question. While Ada ponders, Catsby saunters into the room, growls once at me, and then rubs against Kal's legs. I roll my eyes. Of course Catsby would love Kal immediately. He jumps up on the island and tosses the basket off before Loretta shoos him away.

I peek into the oven as the sugar on the pies begins to slowly evaporate, leaving a shimmery coating behind. In an hour, the apples will bubble and soften, the pie will be golden perfection and the spices will mingle in the air like a rare perfume. It will taste especially good with Loretta's brown sugar vanilla bean ice cream that's undoubtedly in the freezer (although in my humble opinion it's not quite as good as my own cinnamon oat milk ice cream).

Loretta shuts the door after giving Catsby the boot. She sashays over to Kal, eyeing her wavy black locks. "You should get a pixie haircut. It'd be rad. Are the kids still saying that? If you come back on Saturday after school, I'll cut it myself. I'm a bit of a whiz with scissors."

Kal smiles. "I've been growing it long because we

could never afford a haircut. It could be a good time for a change."

Loretta pats her arm. "This town is your home. Embrace it. Being different is the best thing that could happen to you."

Kal looks worried now. "If Esmerelda Diaz doesn't find out about me and whatever I am and lock me up or throw me out."

"Don't you worry about Esmerelda Diaz," Ada says, startling us all. "I think I have the best solution for everyone. But before I tell you what to do, I need a favor."

"Of course," Kal responds right away. Exactly as I told her not to do.

"Good," Ada says, a smile stretching her papery thin cheeks. She crosses over to the bookshelf that houses a million tattered cookbooks and pulls out a butter cookie tin. She hesitates, staring down at it in her hands before setting it in front of us on the island. Her fingers carefully pull at the metal flap until the lid comes off. Kal and I lean closer to peek inside.

Three lockets lay on midnight blue cloth. Something about them feels cold, unusual.

"What are those?" Just being near them gives me the heebie-jeebies.

But Ada doesn't seem to notice my misgivings. "These

lockets block magic from around you. You need protection because the both of you have to go to the Adachi
estate. Winifred, you are connected to the curse and An
Enchanted Match, and only you can undo it. Kaliope, I
need you to look after her, okay?"

"This will be an adventure," Kal agrees.

Recipe Journal of Winifred Mosley

GREAT GRANDMA CATHERINE'S APPLE PIE

Whenever we make this pie, it feels like fall has officially arrived. Now, you don't need magical apples, but they certainly make this pie pop! Magic apples are sparkly, like ruby-red slippers, and make you all warm and happy inside. But if they look just a little too perfect, smell just a little too sweet, they may be poison apples, you know, from an evil witch (which are totally things. Surprising, right?), so be careful! Use regular apples if you aren't sure.

Crust:

2 1/2 cups all-purpose flour

1 cup (16 tablespoons, 226 grams if you're fancy) butter (cold, and divided into tablespoons)

1 tablespoon brown sugar

1 teaspoon cinnamon

1 teaspoon salt

1/4-1/2 cup ice water, which is water with actual ice cubes in it. For real, this is important.

Apple Mix:

8-9 apples (enchanted preferred), peeled, cored, and sliced into 10-12 slices an apple

3/4 cup sugar

2 tablespoons flour

1 tablespoon cinnamon

1 medium dash nutmeg (you know, just shake the
     nutmeg over it once)

2 tablespoons butter

Sometimes I add dashes of ginger, cloves,
     cardamom . . . That's optional, but they do add
     this warming feeling. Like if you're looking out
     the window on a chilly night while the fire's going
     and you're wearing a cable-knit sweater, these
     are the spices for that vibe.

How to make:
For the crust, it's only five steps!

1. Combine dry ingredients and the tablespoons of
   butter.
2. Squeeze the butter with the tips of your fingers
   until it's in pea-size pieces.
3. Slowly mix in ice water with fork until a dough forms.
4. Knead gently into a ball.
5. Chill at least an hour!

For the complete pie:

1. Preheat oven to 350°F.

2. Mix apple slices with flour, butter, sugar, and spices.
3. Divide crust dough into two pieces.
4. Roll out one piece into a big circle large enough to cover the pie pan. Cover the pan but leave the edges for now!
5. Add the apples on top, try to smooth out.
6. Cover the apples with the second rolled-out crust. Crimp the edges with a fork and definitely slit the tops in a pattern to let the apples breathe while baking.
7. Bake for 75-80 minutes, until crust is golden and apples are soft! Cool and ENJOY!

20

Kal

"Y ou're very quiet, Kaliope." Violet's voice carries across the room. *"Do you not wish to talk to me anymore?"*

I turn, letting the tips of my fingers slide down the glass windows, the condensation leaving tiny droplets on my skin. "No, I do. I'm just thinking. I have a lot on my mind."

"What are you thinking about?"

I kick off my shoes, deciding I'm done for the day. I might just sleep through school tomorrow. "About things I have to do. About . . . how hard it is to be me. About how my magic is different and that's bad. About how I'm failing at everything."

Violet is quick to respond. *"Everyone fails. It is the gift of life to fail many times so that you may learn to succeed. And then you will have the determination to never fail again."*

"How would you know—you're just a witch in a book." The anger threads my tone and I hate it. Violet's done nothing but be kind and listen to me. I'm not entirely sure I deserve her friendship.

"I'm not a witch; I'm an enchanter." She audibly exhales. "I may be exiled, but you know I lived a life outside this book. I faced troubles, argued with my parents, made and lost friends, learned to use my power."

I huff. "Power that got you exiled."

"Yes."

I take a seat on the floor, picking at a stray strand of rug that pokes out. I wonder how old it is. Another remnant from whoever lived here before. Maybe it was Violet's. "What exactly is your power? Your enchanter power? You said you're a word enchanter but you haven't taught me any word spells."

"It's a long story, Kaliope."

I fall back on the floor, letting my body settle against the rough material. The room's too bright but I lack the energy to get up now. "I want to hear the story, but first, do you know a spell to turn the lights off?"

"I have a very clever spell, one that's really quite beautiful."

"Just a basic, easy one." I sniff. "There's a witch hunter in town who's gonna lock me up if she finds out I'm not normal, and I don't need any more of her attention."

"A witch hunter can only sniff when she's caught a scent, and I believe she is more concerned about Winifred than you, dearest. But alas, an easy spell . . . Let me think."

Have I ever called her Winifred to Violet before? I'm definitely overthinking it. I'm sure I've mentioned it.

"*Magic to cast the day, magic to cast the night, with these enchanted words, take away the light.*"

The lights flash at her words. Should she even be able to make that happen? I thought magic didn't work for her when she's trapped in a book. No, I must've imagined the lights flashing, because she can't do that. I'm just really tired and emotional, that's all.

I repeat the words, and we're plunged into a comfortable darkness with only the gentle glow of the stars on my ceiling to guide me into bed.

Violet whispers from her book, though she sounds so much closer. "*Let me teach you more spells, Kal. Let me show you magic . . . Let me in. Trust me.*"

The All Hallows' Eve Jumble Sale is the most bizarre thing I've ever seen. It's packed, the main streetlamps have been converted to candles, and strings of fairy lights add an air of magic. People—including a watchful Esmerelda Diaz—meander slowly through the town square sipping their apple cider from Ada and Loretta's orchard, and buying old, and frankly frightening, stuff. I've already seen a massive portrait of a vampire complete with a tiny candleholder at one booth, and a sculpture collection of crows at another. They've been selling like hotcakes. Every other person bought one and strides by clutching this fragile thing to their chest.

Wayward Sentiments has their own booth, which Wini's aunt and dad are working. Wini told them she skipped school yesterday after the incident, which I then also had to admit reluctantly to my dad. Weirdly, no one seemed to care. In fact, Ian cackled and Dad shook his head. Maddie actually seemed happy Wini made a friend who followed her home to keep an eye on her, while Marcus gave me a thumbs-up. Before bed, Dad even said he was proud of me.

Not so sure that'll hold up if we're caught sneaking into the woods late tonight, though. First, however, we have to trade a necklace for a spell. Ada's big favor.

We meet at the statue of Derrick before heading over to Laynie Duncan's booth, who apparently has the counter-spell we need. Wini's holding two steaming cups of hot chocolate topped with brûléed marshmallows. She shoves one into my hand when she sees me.

"The best hot chocolate around, after mine of course, comes from Mindy's Pharmacy off Main Street. She's got this great old-fashioned coffee place that only serves hot drinks, fresh lemonade in the summer, and for some reason, German currywurst. Her booth's over there. Wanna see?" She points to a woman wearing a traditional German dirndl, hair wrapped around her head in a thick braid. She smiles when she sees me.

My gaze swivels to Wini. "You're stalling."

Wini takes a gulp, marshmallow fluff coating her upper lip. "I'm just nervous. Doing magic on the Adachi estate at night, especially at midnight on the eve of Halloween, seems risky."

"I'll be there. What's the worst that could happen?" I thread her arm through mine. People wade by us, gazes fixed on the booths and their wares. The grass is matted but still green. Someone must've come by earlier to blow away the million damp leaves. The breeze is cool but comfortable tonight, and smells of cinnamon-sugar-glazed almonds. A good night for magic, I think.

"Famous last words." Wini chugs the remaining cocoa and dumps her cup into the bin beside a massive pumpkin with a surprisingly elaborate and accurate portrait of Rihanna carved into it.

My stomach makes a sound as we pass a booth selling beignets. This is 100 percent Wini's fault. Before her, I enjoyed sweets, but she made me cherish them. I don't just shove a doughnut in my face anymore—I savor each bite. I'm mindful and I smell things, which is why I decide to buy a brown paper bag full of mini beignets before we leave.

"C'mon, stop being so pessimistic. It'll be fun and

we'll make it work out all right, I promise. But if we don't, blame it on me. Our dads can punish me, okay?" I take another sip of the cocoa. It coats the back of my throat in rich chocolate that's not too sweet. It warms my insides and makes me feel invincible.

"I'm not worried about punishment." She looks down at her boots, her hands fidgeting. "Okay, yes, I'm a little worried about that. But I'm really worried about what could go wrong."

"We'll be okay. We'll end this spell and everything will be just fine. Promise."

"You think so?" She perks up as a group of our classmates passes by whispering about the big Halloween party slash haunted house happening tomorrow night that neither of us were invited to. "Let's go get this spell."

I polish off another beignet, which upsets Wini, as she believes the Mosleys make the best and promised to teach me. Of course, it didn't stop her from taking one. We both have a fine dusting of powdered sugar on our coats, not that we care.

Dangling from the awning of Laynie Duncan's booth are a hundred multicolored shawls, wind chimes, and strands of obnoxious beads that clink together whenever someone walks by. This booth is *the* place to be. Everyone and their mom is haggling over her handmade or vintage costumes, but according to Laynie, the costumes have to "vibe" with the right person. It would seem not everyone's vibing—more people walk away empty-handed and grumpy than not.

Some woman glares at Wini the moment we arrive. She's got jet-black hair and pale, pearly skin, her arms are full of beaded bracelets that look like she made them herself, and she's wearing cat-eye glasses that are seriously sharp at the corners. "You," she tosses angrily our way. "Whenever you're near my arm hurts."

Wini rolls her eyes, shifting on her feet. "It was forever ago, Ms. Chavers. Let it go. I'm sorry about the strawberries."

The lady only glares as she pays for her costume, pushes past us, and gets lost in the crowd.

"What's that about?"

Wini only shakes her head. "Enemies for life. You know how it is."

My brows knit together. "Not really," I mutter, but Laynie has spotted us and is shooing people away.

"Winifred Mosley. Loretta told me you'd be stopping by for a spell?"

Wini doesn't bat an eye even though people gawk at her to see what spell she's buying. She holds her head high. I really wish I had her confidence. She's always herself, for better or worse. Until I came to Honeycrisp Hill, I was always . . . something. I dreamed more often than I did anything. Wini's teaching me that being myself is good.

Laynie rushes off and comes back with a folded piece of paper. When I reach for it, she only tuts, wagging her finger. Right. I slide the third locket onto the counter. The favor Ada asked. She nods once. "There's something you need to know."

"You can only cast this spell on Halloween. And you can only perform it on the Adachi estate." Laynie holds our gazes until we reluctantly nod.

She slips the counter-spell to Wini. Once everything's where it should be, Wini and I high-five. There are still a few hours before midnight and we need to sneak out without getting caught. But we have the solution in hand now, and a plan to boot.

"Kal," Dad says at the same time as Wini's dad calls her name. They share a laugh and stand in front of us.

"You two ought to be off to bed. You have enchantment school in the morning. Ian's home and expecting you right about now." Dad cocks an eyebrow and holds my gaze until I wither under it.

"And you"—Wini's dad points at her—"have been staying up way too late these past few days anyway. I know you love the jumble sale. I'll make sure to get you something special, okay? Maddie'll be there in a half hour to check on you."

I try not to glare at Dad as he and Wini's dad laugh about something or another. I know I should be happy for him, but . . . I guess it kind of hurts to see him so happy with someone else. I shake that thought aside.

Wini and I mutter our okays and head off through the crowds. One booth is selling homemade wolf treats and blood lava cakes. That's the exact wording. I nudge Wini and she only shrugs.

Other booths offer crystal ball, tarot card, and palm readings. One sells enchanted wares that'll make cleaning your house "easy peasy." My eyes catch on so many sparkly things that twinkle in the low light. Full moon pendants, whatever that means. Antique furniture, clocks, books, silverware, champagne flutes, and puzzles. Portraits and landscapes of people and places I don't know but kind of wish I did. Homemade holiday decorations and jars of sand from faraway beaches. None of them make me want to fully stop until there's a booth selling old vinyl records. It takes all my willpower to walk past.

"You ready to get wicked tonight?" I cock an eyebrow at Wini as she unlocks the bakeshop and hits the lights.

"I'm ready to get this spell over with. Wicked's not an option."

"For you," I say, and bite back a smile. Maybe with my different kind of magic, I'm a witch. It still hasn't sunk in yet. But then it does make sense. I can do spells without using my own energy, create where once there was nothing. Like Violet. And though I don't really know what that means going forward, it's good to have an idea. Maybe I'm a good witch, if there's such a thing. Making magic to better the world, even if the Enchantment Agency thinks I should be locked up just for existing.

Unless in order to do the right thing, I have to be wicked.

With a glance back at the town square, I notice Derrick the statue seems different . . . as if he's alive—No. I rub my eyes and turn around. I'm just tired, that's all. I didn't sleep that well, and worse, my room is still unbearably cold despite Dad saying he'd fix it.

I'll take a nap later. Everything will be okay. It'll be better than okay. After tonight, Wini won't have to worry about the Enchantment Agency and we can get back to focusing on magic.

21

Wini

Kal and I collect ingredients—which thankfully are all the things I needed for An Enchanted Match in the first place, plus a few extra items. We carefully place everything in a sturdy knapsack.

"Don't forget to put the spell in there, too," I say, and Kal nods, shuffling things around in her coat pocket. She tosses me one of the silver lockets Ada gave us.

Magic's the only friend I could ever count on. Well, before Kal.

Kal must share some of my suspicion, because she recoils when her fingers touch the center of the pendant. "So all we have to do is wear these and all wicked magic will be repelled from around us? That sounds fake, but okay. We should try them out."

I chuckle, but agree. The center is clear, as if waiting for something to fill it up. I lower it over my head and marvel at the brilliant violet swirling around inside. I peer closer, mesmerized. Kal's necklace shimmers a midnight blue with tendrils of blackness creeping throughout.

"Is this what our magic looks like? Mine's kinda weird, but blue means calm, right?" Her fingers graze the silver.

I nod and reach for mine. "Mine's love." I think suddenly about all the time spent with Aunt Maddie and Dad, practicing spells in the kitchen. Even though we were alone and people hated us for our name and relation to Coraline, we had one another. We still have one another. Their love makes me strong, like magic.

I look over at the television and think of a spell. *"Quiet to loud, darkness to bright, fill this room with noise and sight."*

Nothing happens. Why didn't it work? I'm about to try again when Kal's voice travels over from the banister.

"It's the necklace, remember? At least we know they work." Kal smiles my way. "So we meet back here after everyone falls asleep? It'll be past eleven, but that'll give us plenty of time to check in with our parents and play it cool." She frowns. "Besides, Ian's waiting."

"In two hours, by the woods. We got this!" I sound convincing even to my own ears, though I know it's a lie.

22

Kal

Kaliope . . ." Violet's voice is the first thing I hear
when I'm home in my room. *"There's a different magic
surrounding you. It . . . hurts. It makes me feel ill. Please,
make it stop."*

"Oh," I say, clutching the locket, some revelation
lingering in the back of my mind, though I can't quite
place it. Maybe surprise, since my room feels warm for
the first time. "Sorry, Violet. This locket repels magic
from around us. I'll take it off. It's only for the woods
anyway." The moment I slip it off my neck and place it
on the dresser, I begin to feel dizzy. I touch the tips of my
fingers to the walls for stability.

"Thank you, I feel much better." She sounds perky
again, stronger. *"Do you have the spell?"*

"Yeah," I answer shakily, walking over to her book sitting on the table beside my bed. "We got it. How did
you know?" I shake my head. I don't remember telling
her the grand plan. Fatigue moves through my muscles,
and I just want to drop into the bed and go to sleep for
as long as I can, though I know I only have a few hours.

A haze settles over me that threatens to pull me under. I try to fight against it, but I'm so tired.

Violet's voice is soft and comforting. *"Kaliope, don't you remember?"*

But the way she asks me makes me shiver even more violently. I struggle to switch out of my outdoor clothes into my flannel pajamas. The comforter's tossed back as if inviting me to get warm. I've never felt so frigid in this room. All I can do is lie down under the blankets. Maybe the warmth will reach me.

I just need a nap. That's all.

"What don't I remember?" I shake under the three covers. Even my bones have the chills. My breaths leave a fog in the air.

"Where's the spell, Kaliope?"

"I . . ." I whisper, my eyes shutting on their own accord.

"Remember, Kaliope." Her words seem closer, as if she's standing over me. When I glance up, she's there.

My eyes widen and I gasp. She's *real*.

A real person with that ratty black hair and dark gaze I saw in my dream. She wears a long brown dress, torn in places. She's almost translucent, like the ghost we saw in the woods. I can see my bedroom wall through her. The temperature drops even more. My body quivers. Is she a ghost? What had Wini said about ghosts again?

I try to move but I can't. I'm locked in place.

"Where's the spell, my dear?" Her ghostly hand reaches out and touches my hair, tucking it behind my ear. Her fingers are ice. I attempt to pull away but I can't. "Don't be afraid. Did you get the spell?"

I try to say no, that I put it in the knapsack, but the truth is . . . in the back of my head, I know the spell's still in my coat. Why is it there? Why didn't I put it away? I can recall giving Wini the necklace . . . and then everything becomes hazy.

"My jacket," I say reluctantly as her fingers stroke along my jaw. The cold . . . it's unbearable. I feel it from the tips of my toes to the strands of hair on my head. How is that possible?

"Good girl." Her tone is too sweet, like a rotten apple. She leaves me there to rifle through my pockets. "Ah, there it is. Well done."

"Why?" I ask, my head rolling on the pillowcase.

"Oh, my darling." She breathes frosty air on my face. "Thank you," she says gently. "Thank you for letting me in. Thank you for the energy, and the warmth. For letting me free. You were the best friend someone like me could hope for."

"You're . . . You *are* a witch . . . a-aren't you?" I stammer, my throat closing and feeling scratchy.

She smiles, her skin becoming more and more solid the colder I get. She walks over to my old dresser, batting the locket on the floor, and opens the drawers. "Good you kept this. It was mine, did you know? If you had looked, you would have seen my name carved inside the second drawer. Just there." She points at something beyond my periphery and giggles. "I'm not a witch . . . I'm an enchanter. Now I'm a specter. And you've given me new life. You've given me a body."

The words claw through my throat and lips that want to stay closed. "What . . . are you going to do?"

She peers at herself in the mirror, making pouty lips. And that's when I see that her reflection is mine. She is me and not me. I see her for what she is in front of me, a pale ghost, but in the mirror, she's me. In my pajamas. I should have known she never wanted to be my friend. That she never liked me.

"You're . . . me."

She lets out a giggle. "I'm in your body. Look at your skin."

I blink through the exhaustion and haze, and look at my hand clutching the comforter. Or used to be. My skin is translucent while she's solid. I'm in the bed, I think. The blankets aren't lying on me, they're lying *through* me. I'm nothing.

"Oh, don't you worry. You aren't dead, just a specter. I'll fix it, but first I need to fix the mess that Coraline Mosley made of my first spell. I need to steal magic from the most magical place in town: the Adachi estate. You're strong, make no mistake, but I need more to do what I must." When she looks at me, her cheeks pink at the edges. "When I let you out, you'll like it, I promise. And then we can be together, you and me. But for now, you have to go into the book and rest. Everything will be fine. I promise."

She kisses the top of my head, and instead of ice, it's warm. And I hunger for more. For fire. For everything to be normal again.

She sets the book beside my body on the bed. And like metal to a magnet, I'm drawn to it. Some part of me thinks there's warmth there. Some part of me knows that's where I belong now.

"Go in, Kaliope." She splays open the book. "You won't be in there long."

And I do. My traitorous specter form flies inside. It's dark and lonely but there's a bed in the center of the shadowed room. The bed she slept in.

My eyes close . . .

. . . as the pages close with me inside.

Not Kal

The world is stranger than it once was. People carry tiny technology in their pockets that connects them to the world with a swipe of their fingers. They can listen to music anywhere. Their clothes are less polished, less pressed, more casual than ever. I love it.

I feel free.

So new.

And this body is perfect, a perfect home. Though I'd prefer my own body. Only a few hours stand in my way. Soon, I tell myself. Soon, the power will be mine. I'll get my true body back. I'll change everything.

Kal will be with me.

Yes, it'll be hard to get her to forgive me, but she'll see I had no other choice. I'm doing this for us, for enchanters everywhere. Taking back the power that belongs to us. Siphoning it away from all the foul creatures, until only we enchanters have magic.

And I will be beyond powerful. I'll be *unstoppable*.

I smile into the mirror, grimacing when I catch sight of the book lying on the bed. Kal's inside, withered and cold, asleep and angry.

"Not much longer. You'll see."

I pull a black sweater from the closet. With a kiss to my reflection, I run my hands through her long, knotty hair.

"Tsk, tsk, Kal. You really need to brush your hair more." I shove the hair into a bun at the back of my head, letting wisps fall out, and then place Kal's porkpie hat atop it. It doesn't seem seasonal enough to fit in on this momentous day. *"With my magic, from one hat to another switch, turn this porkpie into a witch."* The top grows into a perfect cone. Ah, magic, how I've missed you. "Now, I've got to go cast this curse. After, we'll both have our bodies back." I cackle. I've been called a wicked witch so long, it only feels right to indulge.

A thick black poncho completes the look, and I feel especially wicked in it. All the better if I need to trick Kal's neighbors until I get to the Adachi estate to dig through the dirt.

Just like the rest of the town, anyone in those woods borrowing—not stealing, really—magic will be punished by the gargoyles. The creatures sit atop their estate on the hill, said to be lethal in their pursuit of justice. That rumor has kept most enchanters off the land, at least in my time, but I don't believe in nonsense.

It's taken me nearly a hundred years to get to the magic deep within the soil, but I'm done waiting.

Coraline tried to keep me from it. But thanks to her daughter, I can finally go past her barriers. Her spell is breaking because of An Enchanted Match and now I can strengthen the curse. Spread it beyond the town.

I grab Kal's ratty purse and shove the book—my talisman—inside.

"You're never too far from me, don't worry." I pat the book as if she can feel it. With a flick of the wrist, I flip the light switch off and gently shut the door behind me.

"This door must stay closed. Let these words bind the lock. None shall open it, none shall knock." The spell leaves Kal's lips with confidence, something the owner of this body never had before. Not in magic, at least. But I'll teach her. She'll learn what the Mosley girl failed to show her.

I smile as I bounce down the stairs. The old man waits at the foot, scowling ever so slightly.

"Kal, where are you going? Do you know what time it is?"

From what I know of Ian Clarke, he's a word enchanter who used to work for the Agency, until he quit. He wants to connect with his son and run a bookstore. Neither of these plans have anything to do with Kal. Probably why he's been rather cold to her. Perhaps he's afraid of her mental illness. Maybe he's worried she's the center of his son's life. That gives me reason to dislike him.

"Why do you care?" I slide past him to the coatrack. Beneath it lay Kal's tragic boots.

The man sighs, a defeated, raspy thing as it were. "Kaliope, I know we haven't gotten off on the right foot, but—"

"But nothing. You have secrets." I edge toward him. "You don't want to tell Father about the Agency, what they made you do? Or why you keep these enchanted books housing the wickedest of witches?" I smile as he backs away from me, seeing something in my eyes that hints at power. Rage. "Oh, don't look so surprised . . ."

His feet catch on an empty cardboard box. I thrust out an arm to keep him from falling, surprised by his frailty.

"How is someone like you strong enough to do magic and hunt witches and yet so weak, you can't even stand on your own two feet?" I giggle. "And you're afraid of a girl who barely knows magic."

Ian's eyes widen before he shrugs off my grip. "Who are you? And what have you done to Kaliope?"

"Kal, silly." I wink at him, taking a seat on the bench beside the staircase and picking up her boot that's in need of cobbling. *"Leather and textile, sole and thread, fix the materials to keep them wed."*

The shoes bind together, the flap no longer open. I smile. Oh, how I've missed enchantment.

"Stop! I know you aren't my granddaughter. You must

be from a book. But not one of mine . . . mine can't possess someone. Who are you and what are you going to do?" Ian reaches for a grimoire from the shelf.

I tsk, tying the laces. "Too late now, old man. Besides—" I stand, taking a quick look around. A long time ago this store was owned by my very traditional parents. They sold books about enchantment, teaching young children all the basic spells, castwork, and recipes for vampires who didn't need to eat humans to get blood. They only needed rare meat every once in a while, and they loved to get fancy in the kitchen.

Our store was all wooden, like now, but less colorful. There were magical clocks on the wall, dinging at different times, whereas here, there are beaded bracelets and books with embossed covers. Lounge chairs and throw pillows. The fireplace crackles in the back. Green landscape pictures hang in little spots and there's a definite smell of cinnamon in the air.

"Besides," I repeat, "your magic's weak now. I can feel it. Did the Agency take it or did you use it all up out of loyalty to them?" I laugh, stepping farther away. "But I like what you've done with the place. My parents would've hated it."

I adjust my poncho and saunter out, casting a spell to keep Ian locked inside the store I always loathed. He can stay in his little haven where he can pretend the

Agency only took his years, not his power. What a sad life he lives. Maybe, just maybe, if he's better to Kal, I'll give it back to him.

The cool air brushes against my cheeks and I let my breath whoosh between my lips. Night has well and truly fallen, lending the square an ethereal glow. The town's trussed up in Halloween decorations. Jack-o'-lanterns sit in every shop window, garlands featuring bats, spiders, ghosts, and witches dangle from every post. Tomorrow is Halloween, but All Hallows' Eve is a perfect time to undo a spell and change things.

And change I will.

My only hope is that I don't run into Winifred Mosley. Power like that . . . she could see through this body to the soul below. But . . . I'll cross that bridge if I get to it. Until then, I add a sashay to my walk. *I'm going to live my best life,* as Kal would say.

People wave and say hello as the jumble wraps up, and I return the gesture. I glance at Derrick, standing there still as stone in the center of town. What a grotesque creature. He was the first casualty of my curse—first and only, because of meddling Coraline Mosley.

I barely glance away when the shadow darkens the sidewalk. I grimace, quickening my pace. This town is falling apart and only I can save it by recasting the curse.

I pass the school and take a left into the woods. An

acorn cracks beneath my heels as I slide through the trees. Darkness cools the air around us. But no bogeymen would be bold enough to enter these magical woods. Not so close to Halloween.

Even the thought of bogeymen makes me gag. Magical creatures are disgusting. They don't belong in this world, but especially this town. And when I finally finish my curse the way it was supposed to go so many years ago, they'll turn to stone like those ugly gargoyles. A smile stretches my cheeks.

While stepping over a thick root, I find myself thinking of Coraline. A shame things didn't work with her.

I laugh to myself as I stop to pluck a will-o'-the-wisp glowing bright blue in the early moonlight. It floats timidly but when I reach for it, it disappears. No matter. My eyes close, and the magic sings inside of me. This body never felt more mine.

Coraline was supposed to be mine, too.

She found the book I was banished inside, like Kal. Every time we spoke, my power grew. I could begin doing spells again. I could use her energy to give me life. One thing led to another and I had her exactly where I needed her: with a spell to take magic from *creatures* and give me *life*.

All I needed was to get to the Adachi estate, suck up all that power waiting for me to get my body back, and I would have been the most powerful enchanter in the world. But Coraline became too difficult. Too old. When I began to manipulate her, she broke free. I never expected her to create the blasted barriers to prevent my curse from reaching completion.

She put all her magic into creating those barriers so that everyone inside of the town would keep their magic—even though it changed them from creatures to enchanters. My curse couldn't spread, and it couldn't siphon away their power. She saved the town—not that they ever knew—and by the end, she barely had an ounce of magic left. All of that, for people who didn't even like her.

The experience taught me a lesson. The more inexperienced the enchanter, the better. The more vulnerable, the easier. And never again will I touch a Mosley. If Winifred is anything like her mother, she's trouble I don't want.

I stare up at the Adachi estate, feeling the power beneath my feet that undulates like an underground ocean. *Finally.* The barrier is still there, too—I feel it tugging at me, but it's a mild feeling. I have to be quick; once the barrier breaks completely, my new curse can take hold if I cast it just right. It can spread with just a few words.

An owl hoots somewhere in the distance as I turn away from the estate and close my eyes, feeling the power beneath my feet. I must find the center of that power and dig into the soil. Once I'm far beneath, I'll be able to do the spell. I'll be able to get my own body back. But first, I need to wait for the clock to strike midnight, for it to be Halloween. When I'll be at my strongest.

And then I'll cast it, taking away all the magic from the creatures; the ghosts, witches, shadows, and anything that's different, everywhere. Forever.

23
Wini

Stevie Wonder's voice croons from my alarm clock. I let out a groan. This spell has got to stop. I love me some Stevie, but this is too much.

My eyes flutter open, but my body refuses to move. The bed is so warm and inviting and I know it's not morning yet. Still, I've got to move. Kal's probably outside waiting for me. Though, after one glance at the clock, I realize it's a bit earlier than I was supposed to wake up. Weird. Using all the energy I can muster, I bolt out of my bed and get dressed.

Only a few minutes have passed till I'm at the front door, knapsack strapped across my back. Aunt Maddie's snoring echoes down the stairs. It doesn't matter that Aunt Maddie is harsh, sometimes mean, uncompromising—she's a great aunt. A great chef. I'm lucky to have her and Dad. It's the thought of him that makes me pause.

He has always been the best dad. And I did a love spell, not to bring him love, but to save our bakery. I want to believe it's because I was keeping Grandma Bernice's dream alive, for Dad and Aunt Maddie, but really, it was for myself.

I called a wickedness to town, played with my dad's love life, caused all this trouble. But we're going to fix it. Me and Kal.

When I step into the cool night, shutting the back door softly, I take a deep breath and look around. Kal's not here. I check my old smartphone and look around again. She's supposed to be here . . . although I did wake up earlier than expected.

A twig snaps somewhere nearby and I jump, my gaze flitting to the woods. There's movement . . . a girl in dark clothing, holding something close to her chest. She runs through the trees. And she looks like . . .

Is that?

"Kal!" I shout, and I touch the locket around my neck, the one that blocks out magic, and shiver. It's warm to the touch, as if it's holding all my magic within it. I don't like it, but it's the smart decision after all those spooky creatures ambushed us in the woods last time.

With a long, deep breath, I trudge into the woods after her, toward the Adachi estate. My heart pumping, I jog through the trees on shaky legs. The faster I get to the center of their land, the faster I'll see Kal again, and the faster we can end the spell. The faster Esmerelda Diaz will leave and I'll keep my magic. Plus, the town gargoyles won't have enough time to come punish us for using Adachi magic if we say our spell quickly and run away. I've never seen them in action, but I *don't* want to see them in action, either.

"Hey, Kal! Wait up!" She's moving too fast. Maybe we said to meet somewhere else? Maybe she's got her headphones on and she can't hear me? I hope she's wearing her locket at least.

A fog thick as molasses settles over the woods like a woolly blanket. As I pick up my pace, I pull a leaf out of my frayed curls and pray there wasn't some insect clinging to it when it plunged from the tree above. Out of the corner of my eye, I catch glowing orbs hovering off the ground and stop in my tracks.

A rush of cold breeze swirls around me as I step gingerly toward them, forgetting Kal for a moment. Just a moment. The will-o'-the-wisps are just balls of blue light to the unenchanted, but to us, they are rare, magical flowers. I'm surprised I can still see them with the locket around my neck, but I'm excited, too. Some say they're enchanters who haven't yet passed on to the other side, that they're stuck between the veil of life and death, while others say they are pure, untamed magic.

Everyone agrees, though, that they're a sign.

Of what? No idea.

I follow the path they lay out for me, each one

disappearing the moment I come close and reappearing farther away. They lead me through the trees and over the heavy thicket. Their light shines so bright, it makes the woods seem a little less scary. Part of me knows I should go, find Kal, but those lights . . . they lure me closer. They whisper things I desperately want to hear.

Come on, Winifred.

A will-o'-the-wisp sits between the edge of the town woods and the Adachi estate's woods. The known and the unknown. I bend down to look at it, expecting it to disappear but it doesn't. I take the necklace off from around my neck and I wait until my fingers stop twitching and my breaths come steadily. Grandma Bernice told me once if ever I should find myself in the presence of wisps, there's a quick spell I can do.

"The moon is bright among the stars, the air through the trees is clear and crisp, with my magic I ask permission to touch this will-o'-the-wisp." The orb shimmers and pings my fingers as though it's electric. I try to pull away but the wisp yanks me toward it.

My skin lights up the same shade of glittery blue. I gasp.

To touch one is rare and incredibly lucky. They only share their brilliance with someone special. Grandma Bernice once said that Coraline must've eaten all the will-o'-the-wisps she could find when she was pregnant with me. I used to laugh, but I wanted to believe her. What if being different is just my brand of brilliance? It made having a town full of enemies slightly better. Only slightly though.

The wisp sharing its light with me makes me feel like maybe I'm going to be okay. That all of this is going to be okay.

Movement through the trees pulls at my gaze again. "Kal, where are you going? Hey!" I dart after her. It's darker and hazier in the Adachi woods, and I'm grateful for the light the will-o'-the-wisp gave my hands. I hold them out before me, letting the light show me the way. "Hey, wait up!" My boot nearly gets stuck under a rock, but I keep moving. I'm closer now, yet she's so fast. "Kal?" I call out.

Something falls from Kal's hands and she bounds off. I huff as my feet stomp through the muck, until I stop briefly to find what she may have dropped.

"Wini?" her muffled voice calls from the . . . ground? *"I'm here . . ."* My heart is pounding hard against my chest and the ground feels alive beneath my feet. *"I'm . . . in . . . the book . . . !"*

"The book?" I stare at her retreating figure and back at the ground. What?

Her voice is still muffled, still close but far. *"I'm . . . in . . . the . . . book! Please find me."*

"YOU'RE IN A BOOK?!" I shout. A patch of moonlight lands on my now-still feet. "What do you mean, you're in a book?" I look around but there's only patches of dirty leaves clumped together, branches, and the creatures that live beneath it all.

"It's . . . a . . . long . . . story."

"Har har." I laugh, though it's not really funny.

The response is slow. *"If . . . there . . . were apple . . . trees around . . . We'd have a pie . . ."*

"This is no time for jokes—wait. Kal, if you're in a book, who's in your body?" I look at the retreating form through the trees.

"Violet. Evil enchanter. Curse maker. Needs power. Bad things coming," Kal says. *"Wini, she's—"*

A branch scratches my arm as I stumble back. Something—the book, lifts off the ground as if it's being called back to the evil enchanter. Oh no, what if it is? This is magic beyond me. "Kal!"

"Wini! Help me!" Kal screams as the book flies off through the woods.

I shout her name and begin running after her. But too soon, Violet disappears through the trees, and the book is too fast behind her. I can't register exactly where I am past the anger thrumming through my veins. I can't see or find her. How am I going to save her? How does a person steal someone's body and put them in a book?

I wait for a sign. My hands still carry the light the wisp gave me, but it's not enough. I don't know where she went. I look up.

The moon is shining, the stars are twinkling, I swear I can smell Halloween candy, and magic swirls around lazily. Where is she? The only friend I've ever had and she's gone . . .

I think back to what she said. *Curse maker. Bad things coming.*

"If she's going to cast a curse, she'll stay close to this estate. She needs power," I say aloud to myself, shifting on my feet, staring out at the dark sky. An Enchanted Match woke me up early, brought me out here. Brought me to the wisps. All to save Kal. She means the world to me. I know that now. Which means I have to stop this evil Violet. If she's going to steal power, she's going to where the power is strongest. And that is . . .

A black fog emerges from the trees and blots out the moon. Whispers echo through the thicket. Hisses and hooves stomping on leaves move around me. The air grows colder. Something wicked this way comes. I reach for my necklace, but it's not there.

I took it off to touch the wisp . . . When I tap my pockets, it's not there, either. I must've lost it.

Oh no.

"Winifred . . ."

My head swivels up to the sky, though it's too dark. The shadow is here, too. I feel her. She's watching me, waiting. And I'm beginning to think she doesn't mean me harm, maybe she's just another part of the spell.

Twigs snap, a wolf howls, and darkness curls around the edges of my vision. My hands clench into fists at my sides. How am I going to get through these woods unscathed and stop Violet in Kal's body?

"Stop right there!" Esmerelda Diaz steps through the trees, her hair disheveled. There's a smudge of dirt across her right cheek, and an orb of light hovers in front of her, guiding her way. "Winifred Mosley, you are under arrest for . . . all of this . . . this mayhem!" she huffs. She crosses the distance between us, leaves squelching under her shiny boots. "Your family can't protect you now."

The orb illuminates her pinched face.

I squint, my head tilting to the side. Frustration prickles on every surface of my skin. "Since you arrived, I've spent all my time trying to not get in trouble with you, when I should have been helping my new friend and . . . and . . . celebrating my greatest achievement."

"Oh, and what's that? Finishing your mother's wicked spell?" Her eyes narrow and lips curl in disgust. The smudge on her face grows in the light.

"No, I . . . um . . . 'accidentally' found a way to break the curse *and* the barriers you and the Enchantment

Agency couldn't . . . and I—" I stop. The dirt blackens and creeps down her jaw and around her chin. "Uh . . . I think maybe there's something wrong with your face?"

"What do you—" She runs a hand on her cheek, black slime coming away on her fingertips. Her eyes bulge. "Oh my . . ."

Whispers waft around us, taunting, angry, scary.

"Do you think you can stop us with a spell?"

"You deserve punishment . . . enchanter."

"Come to me, my pet."

Esmerelda whirls around. *"Heart and mind, body and soul, shimmer bright what hides in sight."*

The air explodes into a black mass that whirls and swirls. These creatures are probably called bogeymen. They—or it—look like something I believed lived under my bed as a kid. My heart hammers and fingers twitch. My mouth hangs open. Oh no, no, no, no.

"This is your doing," Esmerelda hisses, arms suddenly extended in the air. *"Darkness in sight, give me light."* Lightness pierces through the black mass, and momentarily, I think she's done it. That she's strong and I can relax because there's an actual adult here and her experience at enchantment makes me safe. But then darkness only folds in on itself, blurring the trees, blotting out the sky, dulling our senses.

It laughs, its deep, inhuman voice sending goose bumps up my arms. *"You are no match for us, witch hunter."*

Esmerelda stumbles back, her body crashing slightly into mine. *"Darkness in sight, give me light!"*

This time the spell does nothing. The shadows laugh again, and the ground quakes. The trees bend and sway. We're running out of room and time.

"I just . . . I-I have to . . ." Esmerelda stammers. I'm not sure what she has to do but she's certainly not doing it.

"What kills it?" I ask, my voice wobbly, as it encircles us, closing in. The air is cold, and my body yearns to sleep. Just sleep. To let all light extinguish inside of me and join the wickedness. It's where I belong anyway . . .

"Winifred . . ." The wind calls to me. No, not the wind. The shadow.

Esmerelda gasps. "Only light can break through the wickedness! Do something!"

"But I don't know a spell for that," I mutter, my boots sinking into the mud and my breath falling on Esmerelda's back. "I don't know—"

I hold up my hands and the light of the wisps pours out of them. The dark recoils and growls. But it's still not enough to vanquish it.

A spell. A spell. I have to know a spell.

Just then, words begin to whir through my mind.

Something in me does know. Something that makes me who I am, filled with laughter and love because I'm Bernice's granddaughter. Marcus's daughter, Maddie's niece. Maybe I'm just like my mother, and maybe that's not a bad thing right now, because I'm a Mosley, and our magic runs deep. We don't back down.

I close my eyes, the words drifting to my lips. *"With my magic, I do cast, take this wickedness, banish it fast!"*

A blinding purple light spirals around us—a light I created from my own magic. It's vibrant and dark, the color of blackberries. My magic is love.

There's a howl and a groan, and the shadows, the slime, the coldness retreats. It's not gone, it writhes on the ground and on the tree bark, but it can't hurt us. Not now. Not yet . . .

"You . . . you called that here." Esmerelda's voice wobbles as she stares down at the withered darkness that tries to re-form itself with unsuccessful results.

I stand in front of Esmerelda Diaz. "You really believe I called *that*"—I point to the wickedness—"here?"

Esmerelda shakes her head, eyes narrowing. "You did. Whether you meant to is another question."

I stand tall, though I feel small in her presence. "All I tried to do was save my family's bakery. And maybe that changed everything for this town. But I don't deserve to be stripped of my magic or put in magical jail."

Her expression softens, just a little. "That's for the Agency to decide. You have to—"

"No. Right now, I have to save Kaliope Clarke from an evil enchanter who stole her body and plans on doing something really bad. Okay?"

I suck in air, waiting for her to tell me I'm a child or that I don't know what I'm doing. That it's all my fault and I deserve punishment. But instead, she stands there stunned. Her brow furrowed. "Go. I'll hold them off. Don't think this is over, Winifred Mosley."

And just as I'm about to leave to find Violet, a scream pierces the air.

"*Wini!*" Kal's fear tears through me.

24
Kal

I am small and weak and cold.

So cold.

"Sorry for dropping you back there. The Mosley girl surprised me, yet it was only a quick spell to get you back. My magic is strong now, do you feel it?" Her voice is mine but not mine.

"I-I'm cold," I stutter lethargically. The closer I am to her, the smaller I feel, the quieter my voice. "Let me out."

"Not yet. I've just tasted the Adachi magic. I can recast the curse the way it was meant to be, and then I can retrieve my body. Take the magic from the creatures." She jumps down into a hole in the ground. Around her, there are items and tools needed to complete her curse again. "With your help, I'll be me again."

"Why, Violet?" I'm stalling. "Why . . . do this?" The curse is breaking and the more time I take to keep her from the magic, the better chance everyone has.

"Because they condemned me for being different. Called me a witch. I'm no witch; I'm an enchanter. And it took me so long to find someone whose power could free me. Coraline was a failure, but you . . ." Her voice cracks. "You were everything I wanted and hoped for. Once I get my body back, you and I can be together. I like you, Kal."

"*I liked you, too,*" I say, through tears that refuse to fall. "*But I could never be friends with someone who lied to me, who stole my body and left me inside a book. Who plans on stealing magic from good people.*"

"Kal, please. I'm doing this for us."

"*You're doing this for yourself . . .*" The realization slams into my chest. The signs were there from the beginning. The cold. The dark magic. She manipulated me from the beginning because I needed a friend. When I already had one. "*There's no us and there never will be. You're a wicked witch, and I'll do everything I can to stop you.*"

"Kal—" she whines, as if pained. "No."

"I found you." Wini's voice climbs through the trees, breathlessly. "Get out of the dirt. Now."

"I'd rather not." Violet's anger quickly replaces the brief vulnerability. "It was difficult to connect to the Adachi magic, and I'm going to make this world safe for all enchanters. You should be helping me."

There's resolve and a threat in Wini's tone when she comes to stand over the hole. "Violet or whatever your name is, give me my friend's body back and stop what you're doing. Right now. Or . . . else."

Violet holds the book close to her chest and *tsk tsks*, her lips twitching into a wicked smile. "I'm Violet Marie Christophe. Great granddaughter to the founders of Honeycrisp Hill. This town is mine. And with me in charge, I can save your bakery. I can banish anyone who ever treated you wrong. You'll have everything you could ever want, and you'll have Kal back. It's a win-win for everyone."

For a teeny millisecond of a moment, I think Wini might say yes. This is her dream. That bakery means more to her than anything or anyone. Maybe even more than me.

Wini juts out her chin, her voice confident. "Nah."

Violet grimaces. "You are just like your foolish mother. I should have killed her when I had the chance, but now I can—"

Lightning cracks overhead.

Violet peers upward, her teeth—my teeth—gnashing. "We've got company."

And then the shadow looms closer. Only it becomes more and more solid until . . . it's a woman in a long black cloak with knee-high black heeled boots. The brim of her hat obscures her face. "Ah, Violet. I was hoping we'd meet again."

"Coraline Mosley," Violet hisses. "You've gotten old and hideous. And do I detect a weakness in your magic?"

"My magic was being used against you for thirteen years; I'm a bit rusty. But you were still locked in a book and stealing bodies, it would seem." Coraline steps into the moonlight, her red lips shimmering against her dark brown skin. "I did try to tell the Enchantment Agency the true culprit was you, but they were so convinced it was me, they wouldn't even look. They never questioned why the curse still lingered. They never realized it was my magic holding up the barriers."

"It was Violet?" I ask quietly, only to be ignored.

"They've always been fools." Violet laughs. "If they knew you were the one to stop me before I could complete the spell, they would've given you a parade. Such a shame."

"They made me out to be a wicked witch, and that's what I became." Coraline tips her hat upward. I see so much of Wini in her, that it nearly takes my breath away.

"Coraline?" Wini stands there, her mouth open, staring at her mother. "M-Mom? It was you . . . all along?"

Coraline shifts on her feet, something sad flickering in her eyes, but she doesn't get a chance to answer.

"Not that I don't want you to have your little family reunion, but I've got a curse to cast, and I'm not so keen on witches." Violet clutches the book tighter to her chest and lowers a hand into the dirt. "*Adachi magic, woven and sewn, thread and stitch, I demand you, kill that witch!*" Her hand—*my* hand—points at Coraline, and the ground rumbles.

Branches whip out and wrap around Coraline. She doesn't fight it, only smiles as it begins to pull her away, farther into the woods and forest. Wini starts after her, only to stop as Coraline's voice calls out.

"You are strong and powerful, unlike me, Winifred. You can do this!" she shouts over the crackling of tree limbs and the pounding of dirt.

Violet laughs with my mouth, a twisted, ugly laugh. She doesn't sound like me at all. With Coraline gone, she only smirks at Wini. "You next?"

"*Violet, don't!*" I order from my pages. She can't hurt my friend, she can't use my body to do it, I won't let her. I'm a Clarke, and our words have power. "*Don't hurt her.*"

"Aww." Violet runs a finger down the spine of the book. "You'll see it had to be done—"

Wini stands like an Amazon warrior, her voice carrying on the wind. "*Sun and . . . moon, with magic I . . .*"

"*Implore!*" I shout.

"*Sun and moon, with magic I implore,*" Wini pauses, trying to come up with a rhyme. "*From body to specter . . .*"

"*Restore!*" I finish.

"That's right, Kal!" Wini's voice carries all the confidence I wish I had. *"Sun and moon, with magic I implore, from body to specter, restore!"*

"You aren't powerful enough for me!" Violet screams, dirt swirling around us as she hovers off the ground. "You're nothing!"

The wind tears at Wini, threatening to blow her away. But she won't leave. She won't leave me. She's my friend. I'm not alone. Not anymore.

"Sun and moon, with magic I implore, from body to specter, restore!"

Violet smiles, her mouth twisting my features into something truly evil. I hate the way she makes me feel and look. I hate that she used my experiences, my desperation against me. And I made it so easy for her. That ends now.

"Sun and moon, with magic I implore, from body to specter, restore!" The words are hard to say, and they miss the beat with Wini's, who clings to a tree, a look of determination on her face.

Violet hovers above the dirt, arms outreached. *"Heart and soul, body and mind, the perfect match you must unwind. Break the barriers, strengthen the curse. With my magic, the spell reverse!"* Items levitate and glow around us. Violet laughs . . . before everything falls to the ground. Her eyes widen. "I don't understand." Her feet—my feet—plop onto the dirt and she stumbles to gain purchase. "But the spell—"

"You're too late," Wini says as the wind dies down. "An Enchanted Match is done. Like pieces of a puzzle all put together. My mother was the last piece."

My mind whirs.

An Enchanted Match did bring us all together. Ada said it's like a game of chess, and she was right. It moved the pieces around in mysterious ways. Coraline was the last piece. It was about love. It was about friends, like Wini and me. It was about family, like Ian, Dad, and Marcus. It worked . . . it worked against Violet.

"*No!*" Violet touches the spine of the book. "Kal. Don't worry. I—"

I try so hard to put strength into my voice, despite the cold, despite my anger, despite how tired I am. "*Sun and moon, with magic I implore, from body to specter, restore!*"

"Kal, please," she begs, kicking dirt over *my* boots to strengthen her just a little longer. "Your words don't work. You're too weak."

Maybe she's right. I'm a disaster at magic, only half my spells work. I am weak. The loop plays in my mind . . . *You're worthless. You are nothing, mean nothing, no one likes you. You're a joke.*

But Wini's voice cuts through the loop, severing its power in my mind. "Together. We do it together." Wini stands there as wind whips at her curls. She can't see me through the pages, but she feels me. She believes in me.

I find strength knowing Wini's voice will join mine. That we'll do this together. That we're friends and she's here for me. *"Sun and moon, with magic I implore, from body to specter, restore!"*

Violet holds me tighter. "Kal, no."

Wini runs toward us, the air picking up around her as if she's a mighty force to be reckoned with. Her strength gives me strength.

"Sun and moon, with magic I implore, from body to specter, restore!"

We repeat the spell as Violet tries everything to maintain her power over me. She scrambles from the hole, tries to leave, but her path is blocked by Wini, who refuses to budge.

"Winifred. I could still help you. I could still—" But Violet stops. She has nowhere else to go. No one else to manipulate.

With all the strength I can muster, I join Wini one last time. Magic spirals around us, hers a gorgeous purple, and mine . . . a deep, clear blue without any of the darkness. *"Sun and moon, with magic I implore, from body to specter, restore!"*

I'm thrown into the warmth, into my body. Violet,

cold and translucent, reaches out to me as the book begins to suck her inside. I watch her with sadness. I know what she's lived in now for nearly a century. No one deserves that.

Her lip wobbles and silver tears streak down her cheek. "Kal, what about us? We could have been so powerful together."

"I never needed power. I needed a friend." I glance at Wini while swatting my own tears away, but joyful to feel them. To feel myself, every flaw and all. My world may swish between vibrant colors and gray dullness, but it's my world. And there's no place I'd rather be.

She flies back into the pages and I wait, just to make sure she's still there, before running to Wini and collapsing into her arms.

Violet is in her book where she belongs, and Wini and I walk back through the woods together. The town's barriers are broken and the curse is gone, all thanks to Wini and An Enchanted Match.

"That was ninety-nine percent bad," I admit, sliding a glance to Wini. "We could have really gotten in big trouble there."

Wini laughs a little, though her mind seems elsewhere.

Like on her mother who suddenly appeared and left again. "Speak for yourself, there's no way I'm not grounded for a year."

"Better that than losing your magic, getting thrown in jail, and—"

"How did you meet her, Kal? Who was Violet?" Wini squeezes my hand, sliding me a glance.

I let out a deep breath that fogs in the air. A moment passes before I tell her all about the girl in the book who listened to me, cared about me, showed me magic, made me feel like I belonged. And every time I was scared, like when I found out my magic is more food magic than word magic, Violet told me it was okay even if the Enchantment Agency might say differently. I liked her. I *liked* Violet.

Wini stops, but doesn't let my hand drop. "You know I'm always here for you, right? You are going to make more friends, find your way through magic, and lots of good things are going to happen. Some bad, too, but you and me, we're friends. I'll be there for all of it. So will our dads and Aunt Maddie, Ian, and—"

"I know," I say, wiping a tear from the corner of my eye. "I know that now."

She's about to say something more when arms are thrown around the two of us, pulling us apart.

"Kaliope Clarke, what have you done?" Ian's whispers

land somewhere between my hair and my ear. "Where were you? Are you okay? Are you still someone else?"

"Ian, I'm—" He holds me so close, I'm enveloped in a teddy-bear hug. And I don't mind it at all.

"I was so worried about you." He sniffles. "My only grandchild . . . knowing you and Lachlan were waiting for me once the Agency finally let me go was the only thing keeping me going. If anything happened to you . . ." His voice trails off.

"*Winifred Theodora Mosley*, you've got some explaining to do." Wini's dad stalks through the trees alongside my dad, Aunt Maddie, and a whole crew of townspeople holding flashlights. As I peer a bit closer, I clutch Ian a little tighter. The people look different. Fangs flash, and whiskers poke through fur-covered creatures that were once normal-as-pie townspeople. Some still have usual hues of skin, but others are green and blue and all kinds of colors. These are their true forms—this is what the curse must've taken away from them. I'm mesmerized and then I realize, I need my best friend—the person responsible for all of this—to feel tethered to this new world.

I reach out and grab her hand as our families crowd around us.

She smiles and then looks at the townspeople, surprise in her gaze.

"Thank you," Mr. Collins says, stepping toward me

into the moonlight with someone I can't quite place but seems familiar, on his arm. I notice the shine of his pearly white teeth before I see the sharp tips of his canines. My eyes flash up to his.

I shake my head as a cool breeze seeps through my jacket. Maddie throws her thick plaid poncho over my shoulders, rubbing my arms in the process.

"We . . . I'm sorry . . . We're sorry. We've been afraid for so long, and trapped." Mr. Collins's gaze darts between me, Dad, and Maddie, and finally lands on Wini. "Derrick and I can't thank you enough."

Before any of us can speak—Derrick's not a statue anymore?!—another woman steps up in front of Wini. "How can we ever thank you?" She's covered in deep green scales and has bright, neon pink lips. She's intensely cool.

All these creatures, townspeople I've never known but Wini has, surround us. They aren't enchanters. They're wolves and vampires and all the things I've ever read about in fairy tales. They're real, just like ghosts. This world is getting bigger and more interesting, and I'm a part of it.

Ian coughs, pointing toward Esmerelda Diaz, who trips over a tree branch in the clearing, her eyes locked on mine before sliding to Wini's. Her fancy, modern dress is askew, and twigs poke out of her hair. She doesn't look at all happy to be here.

"This is illegal. All of you . . . you creatures, are in violation of the rules." Her voice rises high like an angel food cake, only nothing about it is angelic. "And you"—she glares at Wini—"you are at the heart of this. I spared you earlier, but now I know you're a witch just like your mother—"

"Not all witches are wicked, Esmerelda," Ian says with a hint of sadness. "You thought it was suspicious I left the Agency after so long, but the truth is, I couldn't watch more witches suffer just because their magic was a little different than what we were told was right. We shouldn't be hunting them; we should be including them."

Esmerelda's mouth flops open, so I shove Violet's book into her chest.

"And I think you'll find the culprit here. She's the original wicked witch." I lift my chin to look in her eyes. "You owe both Coraline and Wini Mosley apologies."

Esmerelda holds the book out, and Violet weakly murmurs something about letting her out. "I see. Well . . . I'll have to run this by the Agency and we will—"

"Leave us alone, at least for now?" Dad asks, staring Esmerelda down. "It is Halloween, after all, and it seems that when you have a whole town in the middle of the woods, it's a good place and time as any to have a party."

Esmerelda shakes her head as people step past her. "I will be back, mark my words."

"We look forward to your public apologies," Loretta says in a fabulous turquoise ballgown with her arm wrapped around a smirking Ada.

Esmerelda scowls and tries to say something else, only we all drown her out with cheers and whoops. She mutters and stomps off.

"See?" Dad twists in front of Marcus. "All we need is love."

"All we need is love," Marcus repeats, and I swear his dark brown cheeks blush, or at least climb a few degrees despite the chilly weather.

"Wrong band," I huff, and then take Dad's phone from his pocket. I hit a few buttons, and soon Stevie Wonder's "Isn't She Lovely" trickles out. Wini groans, which we all ignore.

"*Music too soft to hear, make it loud, make it clear!*" Maddie casts, and the music fills the woods around us. People clap and pat her on the back.

Marcus looks up, lips pinching at the sides. "*Darkness in the dead of night, from above, nature give us light.*" Trees bend their branches down toward us, their leaves glowing in the moonlight. People *ooh* and *ahh*, including me. I've never seen him do magic, but I'm guessing I will from here on out.

Dad slowly steps toward him, cheeks a bit pink. "*Lachlan and Marcus stood in front of each other, their eyes round like the moon above. The sweet sounds of Stevie Wonder and the town filtered around them . . ."* Just then a warm breeze caresses my cheeks. *"And everyone began to dance."*

The world around us shimmers and brightens with all sorts of colors. Dad and Marcus embrace each other and dance much slower than the beat. Maddie sighs, and Ian smiles.

Wini looks over at me. "I told you, lots of good things are going to happen. And we're going to be here through it all. You aren't alone."

Coraline Mosley walks up beside us, her hat askew. "Looks like I have a lot to catch up on."

Wini's eyes widen. "Are you going to stay?"

Coraline smiles. "There's no place else I'd rather be." She lifts a gloved hand and sparks fly out. "It sure does feel good to have my magic back . . . and my family."

I nudge Wini with my shoulder. "Family."

25

Wini

I set my empty plate on the counter besides the remnants of the massive roast chicken, mashed potatoes with at least a cup of butter, collard greens with bacon, cheddar pesto bread cut into cubes to sop up the thick chicken gravy waiting in a porcelain boat, Grandma Bernice's famous candied purple yams, honeyed corn bread, and roasted carrots topped with fresh parsley. It was a feast. And why wouldn't it be? We have Ian, Lachlan, Kal, and Coraline over for dinner.

I have a feeling this will be a weekly thing. Or maybe even nightly if things go well between Dad and Lachlan, who began dating the moment Kal gave her blessing.

With one glance though, I can see there's no *if*, only *when*. Their eyes lock on each other's. Lachlan's elbow is on the table, leaning into Dad, whose breathless laugh adds to the harmony and music. Which happily is not Stevie Wonder. Not that I don't still love him, but we've all heard enough for at least a little while longer. Instead, it's Lachlan's choice: Aretha Franklin.

They laugh and talk about whatever old people talk

about. Probably getting enough fiber or whatever. Or Ian's new job helping witches come out of hiding or the battle against Violet outside the Adachi estate, as if it hasn't been talked to death.

The bell over the door jingles once as Ms. Chavers taps on the glass, holding the copy of *You've Got Mail* I left in her mailbox. There's a smile in her eyes but a scowl on her lips. Okay, so maybe not everything changed.

I watch her disappear down Main Street before taking a seat beside Maddie and Kal, who talk about school and all the magical creatures wandering around town. Ian's writing down his recipe for shortbread, and Coraline reads Grandma Bernice's grimoire of experimental magic.

The curse is over. Esmerelda Diaz took Violet's book and cleared Coraline of all wrongdoing.

Coraline never abandoned us. Never hurt anyone. Instead of running, she locked herself and her magic into the barriers shortly after I was born and kept the town safe from the curse. Kept Violet from succeeding for a long time. The Enchantment Agency gave her a medal and offered her a job, which she politely declined. She wants to spend time with her family. She wants to get to know me, and I think maybe I'd like to get to know her, too. All in all, I'd say this was a win.

Now that the town knows the truth, they held a fund-raiser to pay off our bills and keep us from bankruptcy. Which was fine and good, but their apology—which included another flash mob dance—almost made up for the years of anger.

Almost.

Thankfully, business is better than good. Mr. Collins and Derrick, who is no longer a statue but a living, breathing vampire, gave us some of their favorite vampire snack recipes and promised us a weekly catering gig for Derrick's card-playing club: *Fanged and Dangerous*. Once we collected his recipes, other creatures followed suit. We started making treats specifically for them. Honestly, I can't wait to start experimenting on blood-soaked chocolate baba, brainy mousse tarts with maybe a bit of rhubarb or raspberry, and wolf biscuits.

"Wini, are you listening?" Kal cocks an eyebrow, taking a big bite of mashed potatoes with a dollop of gravy floating on top.

"Eh, nope." I give her my most forgiving smile. "What were you saying?"

"I was saying, I'm going to try out as Dracula for the school play." She bites on her bottom lip, a blush blooming on her cheeks. "That's if there aren't any actual vampires trying out for the part."

Tons of creatures moved in and out of town the

moment the barrier was broken. Honeycrisp Hill is hopping; strangers walking down our streets, real estate being bought and sold within days, and don't even get me started on the influx of events. With everyone free to be themselves, people seem a whole lot *happier*. And they all seem to like me a whole lot more.

I smile at her. "I think you'll be perfect, and if anyone tries to take your part, we'll—"

"Winifred," Maddie says, lips bunched. "Don't finish the sentence."

"What?" I smile. "I'm just saying we'll make sure she gets the part."

Coraline nods, smirking. "I'll help, too."

"Mm-hmm," Maddie says, which everyone knows is Black for *nope*. "No witchy business."

Coraline smiles as she rolls her eyes. "Anyway, did you hear about . . ."

She and Maddie begin gossiping—apparently a family trait—as Dad walks by.

"What's for dessert?" Even though we work around sweets all day, even though we just had the biggest dinner in the history of Wayward Sentiments, dessert is important. It's our *thing*. It's a gift, an act of love. And dessert is the best act of love we can give to each other.

I imagine what we'll have. Something hot and

chocolaty? Something spicy and fruity? Or something rich and topped with vanilla ice cream? *Mmmmm.*

Suddenly, a wild wind blows, rattling the windows. The lights flicker on and off. Just then, a shadow travels up Main Street.

The streetlamps explode, leaving only darkness. The fake tea lights we left on the counter after chucking the rotten pumpkins turn on, giving us enough weak light to see in.

Dad and Lachlan clamber to the window, staring outside at nothing but the howling wind, leaves, and broken glass.

"Stay there," Lachlan commands. "There's something outside."

I stay plastered to my chair. None of us moves, none of us speaks. Even Maddie is temporarily stunned. Please tell me it's not more wicked things intent on eating our magic, because I've had enough of that for a while.

"Is it a wicked witch?" Kal's voice is low, riddled with fear. "No offense," she says over her shoulder at Coraline . . . *Mom.*

Coraline laughs. "Wicked, my dear, is just another perspective." She saunters to the window, startling Dad, who nearly jumps into Lachlan's arms. "No, it's just a bit of different magic. Should I go handle it?"

"No," Kal and I say together, and then laugh.

"This whole town is magic; what's a bit more?" Kal shifts in her seat and taps the chair beside her for Ian. He nods, the corner of his lips quirking. "Let's let someone else handle it."

"Exactly," I say brightly, flashing Dad a wink. And then I look at all the unlit candles. *With my magic I do implore, enchant this flame, make the fire roar.* The candles all burst into light, their flames whooshing up and then dying back down to a little ball of fire.

Coraline takes a seat beside me and touches my arm. "You're pretty powerful already, but I can teach you some spells . . . if you like."

"Maybe later?" I ask as Dad and Lachlan slide plates of hot chocolate bread pudding in front of us. Kal *ooohs*. "First, let's eat."

Dear Reader,

A long time ago, when I was around the same age as protagonists Wini and Kal in this book, I lived in a small town in Massachusetts that had little apple orchards and brooks weaving through the grass and streets. My family and our apartment was small, but we had a big community just beyond our front door.

That community helped us when money was tight and we weren't sure if we could afford the heat bill come winter. I began babysitting, cleaning houses, polishing silver at the local antique store, and shoveling snowy driveways. As I was looking around town for new jobs, I met an older neighbor who lived alone and had an orchard in her backyard. She said climbing ladders to pick the apples had become impossible for her and asked for help. She couldn't pay me with money, but I could keep as many apples as I liked. And I thought, that's the best deal ever!

Suddenly we had a lot of apples. So I opened up my grandmother's old Betty Crocker cookbook. On a splattered, crinkled page, worn from overuse, I found an apple pie recipe. I asked my mom to teach me, though she had a few tweaks: double the cinnamon, use different types of apples, and don't forget a pinch of nutmeg!

Apple pie became our tradition. We made so many, we gave some to our neighbors—to the library, our friends, and family. Making those pies with my mother made me feel warm, loved, and magical. I'd always liked baking, but at that moment, something clicked into place. I wanted to become a baker, and apple pie was the catalyst. That recipe is in this book.

As you settle down into the story, maybe you can take a break and make the pie with someone you love. You can eat it hot from the oven with a scoop of vanilla ice cream like my mother enjoyed, or the way I like it: cooled down till the inside is solid but soft with a mug of apple cider.

Or maybe you'll make the hot chocolate, blueberry muffin bread, my riff on chocolate chip cookies, or biscuits while you find out just how cursed Honeycrisp Hill is and what Wini and Kal plan to do about it.

Either way, I hope you'll feel warm, loved, and magical while reading this book. I hope you'll enjoy the story that's as delicious as an apple pie.

Thank you,
Alechia

✧ ACKNOWLEDGMENTS ✧

Creating magic—just like making two massive apple pies in one hour!—takes a lot of work, but thankfully, I had the best help.

Many thanks to:

Natalie Lakosil, who helped me find my middle grade voice and believed in this story from the beginning. You cast many spells in the publishing world, and I'm beyond grateful for your expertise and compassion.

Emily Settle, who took a chance on Wini and Kal and gave me all the guidance to break the curse on Honeycrisp Hill. You are an incredible editor, kind and thoughtful, and working with you has been a joy! Thank you, Emily!

The team at Feiwel & Friends, including Avia Perez, Hayley Jozwiak, and Jacob Sammon, for helping me polish this book, you all are the best! And thank you to designer Meg Sayre and artist Lissy Marlin. I will cherish this cover forever; it's absolute perfection.

Tracy Badua, my friend, writing partner, and the person who reads every book from the first draft to the last. Working with you over the years has made me a better storyteller, and I'm so excited to have all of your books on my shelves, including ours, too!

Rachel Somer, Tamara Mataya, Sheena Boekweg, and Leanne Schwartz, who offered me their time into the late and early hours, who have listened and helped me hone my craft. Thank you all, I wouldn't be here without you.

To the best support group out there: Bethany C. Morrow, Jess Sutanto, J. Elle, Tori Bovalino, Anika Wegner, Kendell Penington, Eric Smith, Laura Namey, Mara Rutherford, and Adiba Jaigirdar. You've all spent an extraordinary amount of time listening to me, giving me advice, and answering my questions, and I appreciate it. I appreciate you and your friendship.

To the middle grade authors before me who opened the door for diverse stories in this industry (too many to name, but here's a few): Claribel Ortega, B. B. Alston, Kwame Mbalia, Dhonielle Clayton, Erin Entrada Kelly, A. J. Sass, Kacen Callender, and Janae Marks. Thank you!

To the Milford Town Library, my home away from home. Thank you for giving me the loveliest place to grow up, for making me feel safe, and replacing my library card even though I lost it so many times. It was one of the best experiences of my life working with you all, and you've helped make me into the person I am today.

To my mother, Catherine, my grandmother, Bernice, and my dad, Jeffrey. Thank you for the love, believing in me, and raising me to enjoy (and make) the very best food. I still remember the afternoons in the kitchens, slicing, peeling, stirring, whisking, and tasting. I remember the music, Stevie Wonder (also big thanks to Stevie Wonder!), and dancing. Thank you for the memories.

To Christoph and Liv. Who let me write through dinner, ate pizza once a week instead of my elaborate menus, who let me read this aloud and offered thoughts. You are the best family I could have asked for, and every day I'm excited that I share my life with the both of you. And, Liv, I'm proud of you always and it's an honor to be your mom.

To librarians, readers, teachers, book bloggers, BookTokers, bookstagrammers, reviewers, the entire book community—the only reason I get to keep writing stories is because of you. You've boosted my work, you've shouted from the rooftops, you left reviews and sent me messages. You might not know this, but whenever I questioned whether or not I was good enough, your kind words gave me the strength to keep going. Thank you all.

Thank you for picking up this book.

THANK YOU FOR READING THIS FEIWEL & FRIENDS BOOK.
THE FRIENDS WHO MADE

Just a Pinch of Magic

POSSIBLE ARE:

JEAN FEIWEL, PUBLISHER

LIZ SZABLA, VP, ASSOCIATE PUBLISHER

RICH DEAS, SENIOR CREATIVE DIRECTOR

ANNA ROBERTO, EXECUTIVE EDITOR

HOLLY WEST, SENIOR EDITOR

KAT BRZOZOWSKI, SENIOR EDITOR

DAWN RYAN, EXECUTIVE MANAGING EDITOR

KIM WAYMER, PRODUCTION MANAGER

EMILY SETTLE, EDITOR

RACHEL DIEBEL, EDITOR

FOYINSI ADEGBONMIRE, EDITOR

BRITTANY GROVES, ASSISTANT EDITOR

MEG SAYRE, JUNIOR DESIGNER

AVIA PEREZ, SENIOR PRODUCTION EDITOR

FOLLOW US ON FACEBOOK
OR VISIT US ONLINE AT MACKIDS.COM.
OUR BOOKS ARE FRIENDS FOR LIFE.